CW00816237

The Girl Knows Nothing

The Girl Knows Nothing

KT Cavan

The Girl Knows Nothing
By KT Cavan

Published by Asp
An imprint of IndieBooks

ISBN: 978-1-908041-72-2
© 2021 IndieBooks Limited

Set in Times 11/12
Cover design by Jem Butcher
Cover Illustration by Jacqueline Bissett

Printed by TJ Books Ltd, Padstow PL28 8RW

1

For thirty-six long and sleepless hours, Clemency had dreamed of this. A wide, deep bath, to wash away the journey. Thick curtains to keep out the sunlight and the noise of the traffic. The bed, with its deep mattress and crisp white sheets. Now it was real. They had even turned back the covers and left a rose on the pillow.

She turned away. It was so tempting to lie down and rest, even for a minute, but that would have to wait. Throughout the flight to Idlewild, then south with VARIG to Rio, the delay in fog-bound Montevideo, she had thought constantly of Peter, now in the hands of the KGB. He was the reason she was on this mission, and she forced herself to think what he would do now.

Feeling self-conscious, she looked behind the pictures and the headboards for microphones, and even climbed on a chair to inspect the chandelier. She used her nail file to unscrew the base of the hotel telephone, though her training hadn't extended to electronic eavesdropping and she couldn't be sure if the wires inside had been tampered with or not. Then she checked that the locks on the windows were secure.

And here was another distraction, for the whole of Buenos Aires was laid out beneath her. Wide avenues, gleaming apartment blocks, cafes and markets, the teeming traffic, trams, buses, everything so different, stretching away as far as she could see.

For now, though, all she could do was look. Her instructions were to wait in her hotel room to be contacted. Instead of the city, she explored the bathroom – almost as big as her whole flat back in Bern – and played with the futuristic shower fittings until they produced jets of steaming water. There were white towelling robes and fancy toiletries. She hoped the Office hadn't messed up the booking, and that she wasn't expected to try and claim this on her expenses. This was not the kind of room – or hotel – for a lowly cypher clerk.

She had a long bath and was wrapping a towel into a turban round her head when there was a knock at the door. She half-expected someone from the management, come to check that the room met with her approval. But the man was too well-dressed, too handsome and too arrogant for that. Broad shoulders, dark hair slicked back, except for a lock that had slipped forward; a very good suit, light-weight and English. His eyes were amused, but there was a hint of cruelty there as well.

Something in his gaze led her to look down, to where he held a pistol pointing at her heart.

He gestured with the gun for her to step back into the room. She obeyed, her hand to her mouth. Soon he had backed her into a chair. He sat on the end of the bed and rested the gun on his knee.

She wasn't scared, just furious with herself for being so careless. And with the man, for the way he was looking at her body, what he could see of it; and imagining what he couldn't. For now, though, there was nothing she could do. Not while he held the gun.

'Did you see the article in the *Times* about that polar explorer?' he said.

His voice was English, public-school, rather pleasant. But the words made no sense.

'Who are you? What do you want?'

'The article in the *Times?*' he repeated. 'The polar explorer?'

'I've no idea what—'

Before she'd finished, he'd grabbed her arm and twisted it up between her shoulder blades, then dragged her onto the bed. She lay face-down with his knee in her back.

'Who are you?' he demanded.

'Get off me you… you… shit!'

The pressure on her arm eased. He was laughing.

'You're the real thing, aren't you?' he said. 'Only young English women who've been to the right schools swear like that. Roedean?'

'Malvern,' she replied sullenly, rubbing her wrist.

'So you're Clemency White. Why didn't you give the right response?'

'No-one told me anything about that.'

'Really? The usual cock-up. Anyway, get some clothes on.' He sat down in the chair facing her. 'Don't worry. I won't look. In fact, I've already seen quite enough.'

Her face burning, she wrapped the robe close round herself, chose some clothes almost at random from her case, and retreated to the bathroom. She was shaking, hating him for humiliating her like that. It wasn't necessary. The gun was just play-acting, designed to put her in her place.

She regained some composure as she dressed, applied a little make-up, brushed her hair. If he had to wait, so be it.

But he didn't seem at all put out by the delay. She found him lying on her bed, smoking a cigarette, eating one of the apples from the complimentary fruit basket and reading her diary.

'Fascinating stuff,' he said cheerfully. 'But not ideal from the security point of view. You'd better destroy it.'

'What's your name?' she asked coldly, snatching it from him.

He lay back on the bed, trying to blow smoke rings.

'Hal Linklater.'

In the short briefing she'd had before being rushed to Heath Row to catch her flight, she'd picked up that Hal Linklater was one of SIS's most highly regarded officers; a view to which he clearly subscribed. The first impression of charm and arrogance had been spot on, but she could see there was some humour there as well. He was certainly good-looking. A pity he knew it with such certainty.

'Eyeing the merchandise?' he asked, not taking his eyes from the ceiling.

'How did you get that scar?'

'Here?' He touched his cheek. 'I ought to say it was a fight with a KGB agent while rescuing a top atom scientist from Siberia. In fact, it was coming off my bike when I was fourteen. What about your scars? Maybe we could look for them later.'

'Does this lame comedian routine come for free? I'd hate to think I was paying for it.'

'Oh, ho! The girl has spirit. I must try another approach.'

'Don't bother. I'm already attached.'

'Good thing I didn't shoot you,' he said casually. 'It took a hell of a lot of nagging to get London to send you out here in the first place. Ah, a hint of a smile. I thought you'd see the funny side in the end. And we're going to be working together. *Pax?*'

The childish Latin term reminded her of her brother and his friends. Perhaps Hal thought pointing a gun at someone was all a bit of a joke. But she'd volunteered for this assignment. He'd reached out his hand, and there was nothing else to do but shake it.

'That's the spirit. I'd better fill you in before we see Catsmeat. That's Jacob Pryce-Jones, who's the Counsellor at the Embassy here. I call him Catsmeat – not to his face, of course – because he's stepped straight from the pages of P G Wodehouse. He's running this operation. Or did you know that?'

'I don't know anything. They just gave me a ticket and put me on a plane.'

'The usual shambles. We don't even have a summary of your file yet. I presume you have typing, shorthand and so on. You really are a cypher clerk, aren't you?'

Even if he hadn't intended to be crushing, that was how it felt. She was thinking about the kind of work she had done for Peter in Bern, meeting agents and picking up secret tapes. Hal wanted someone to take notes and send telegrams back to London.

'Do you speak Spanish?' he asked.

'I can get by.'

'What do you know about Argentina?'

'Corned beef.'

'Anything else?'

'The tango, rounding the Horn…'

'Cape Horn's in Chile, but that's close enough. What about Adolf Eichmann?'

'The Nazi? The one the Israelis kidnapped?' She could remember the headlines, the pictures of his trial in Jerusalem. The Argentinian government had refused to extradite him, so the Israelis had snatched him and smuggled him out of the country.

'Are we here to hunt Nazis?'

'That would be too easy.' Hal threw his apple core into the bin on the far side of the room and looked much too pleased that it was a direct hit. 'There are hundreds of them here, and more in Paraguay and Brazil. We're here to find three in particular.'

'Who are they?'

'For now, all you need to know are the three code names: Faith, Hope and Charity.'

'What do we do when we find them?'

He laughed.

'I like your confidence in my abilities, Miss White, but finding them won't be quite that simple. They'll have new identities, the best false papers that money can buy. They may have had surgery to change their appearance. They could be anywhere across hundreds of thousands of square miles. Argentina is the same size as the whole of Europe. Or they may have gone on to Brazil, Paraguay, Bolivia. The only real lead we have is that one of them is living in what they call an *estancia* – a kind of cross between a farm and a country estate – in the province of Misiones, up on the Paraguay border.'

'That's not much to go on.'

'No. I'm going there next week undercover. I'll be a rich younger son travelling with my fiancée and looking for a farm to buy. That way I can go anywhere and ask lots of questions. My line is that England's finished, too much taxation, too many rules and regulations, the future's in South America, that kind of thing.'

'That sounds convincing.' Clemency had heard the same thing said many times, not least by her father and his friends, though usually it was Australia or Canada where they talked of starting again.

'It had better be. If they suspect anything, it's a very long way from Buenos Aires up there, let alone London. No calling in the heavy squad as back-up. And these people are pretty ruthless.'

'What—'

She stopped as Hal stiffened, listening intently, his hand on the butt of his gun. Then there was a gentle knock at the door. He slipped off the bed and nodded to Clemency to answer it, while he stood to one side, out of sight.

'Who is it?'

'I'm a friend of Mr Linklater's,' a voice replied. Hal relaxed and put the gun away.

The man Clemency let in was a young-looking fifty, very tall and thin, with a long chin and round, metal-framed glasses. He wore a dark grey three-piece suit and a white shirt with a particularly high collar that he must have had made specially, the style was so out of fashion. She could see what Hal meant about the characters in the Wodehouse books that her brother liked but that she'd never got on with; except that, despite looking a little like a haddock, Pryce-Jones was clearly intelligent.

He looked her over, then glanced around the room and nodded to Hal. He didn't offer to shake her hand.

'I was just explaining a bit of background to Miss White.'

'How long will we be away?' she said eagerly.

'Away?' Pryce-Jones asked. 'Where?'

'On the Paraguayan border. I thought…'

She trailed off as Hal and Pryce-Jones exchanged glances. Then Hal began to laugh.

'Did you think you were coming too?'

'But you said you'd have your fiancée with you, and I thought—'

'I'm afraid that position's taken,' Hal said. 'I'm flattered, of course.'

'I didn't mean—'

'London is sending out a properly trained agent for that.' Clemency couldn't decide if Pryce-Jones's chilly disapproval was worse than Hal's smirk. 'She'll be here at the end of the week. Your role should be finished by then.'

'What we need you to do is to go through some files,' Hal explained. 'We know that the three men we're interested in entered Argentina between 1946 and 1949. Almost certainly they had forged papers, but there's just a chance that one of them had to use their real name. That could be a useful lead.'

'Where are the files?'

'In the archives of the Federal Government's Immigration Department. They're in an old warehouse down by the docks. Obviously, we can't make a formal request for access, as someone would immediately tip off the ones we're after.'

'How do I get in?'

'That's your job. London said you knew about all breaking and entering.'

For a moment, she had no idea what he meant. Then she remembered the climb up to the study in the townhouse in Bern; the narrow, dusty lift shaft; the fear when she was on the point of being discovered; the exhilaration when she escaped.

'I assumed that's why you packed those slinky black clothes,' he went on, highly amused. 'The professional catburglar never travels without them.'

'You went through my bags?'

'Of course. In this job I don't take any risks, including with inexperienced girls who think they're being helpful. I suppose you could say they are for dance lessons or something. Anyway, once you're in, security is pretty lax, so you'll have the run of the place each night. There are something like half a million landing cards stored there, so it may take some time.'

'The crucial thing is, no-one must find out that we're interested,' Pryce-Jones said coldly. 'It could ruin the whole mission. You simply must not be caught. And if you are, you must keep us out of it.'

Hal tried a more supportive tone.

'Your cover is that you're young and ambitious and want to break into journalism. You think that, if you can get access to these archives, you might find the scoop of the century – proving that Adolf Hitler escaped to Argentina after the war.'

'That's ridiculous.'

'Yes, but you're a very naïve girl. Someone you met at a party in London suggested it to you, and you borrowed the money to come out here.'

She thought it through in silence. It was possible, she supposed. Maybe the Argentinian police would swallow it. Better not to be caught in the first place.

'When do I start?'

'Tonight, so you might want to get some sleep,' Hal said. 'I'll pick you up at ten o'clock and we'll make our first reconnaissance. Then you can get started properly tomorrow.'

'Who am I looking for?'

'What I'm going to tell you is highly confidential,' Pryce-Jones said, brushing a speck of dust that only he could see from his knee. 'Though your own role is something any competent clerk or secretary could do, there is a connection to a mission of considerable sensitivity, which is why we asked London to provide someone to assist. It's vital you take the need for secrecy seriously, including on your return to London.'

'Of course.'

'This, er, cloak and dagger stuff is something of a departure for us. Working for the Office, you'll know that we don't usually like to be drawn into these kinds of matters. Our task is to promote understanding between nations, not cause ruptures. But the circumstances are unusual and we must be prepared to tear up the rule book.'

She struggled to keep a straight face. He was so precise, so mannered, that it was hard to imagine him so much as returning a library book late. He looked at her dubiously but saw no alternative to pressing on.

'Let me begin with the context. In the latter stages of the war, a number of refugees from Communism were offered safe conduct and a new start here in Argentina. For example, there were former officers of the Royal Yugoslav Army who, had they been handed over to the Communist partisans, would certainly have been summarily executed.

'Mostly it was organised either by the Vatican or by the Red Cross, and so all above board. But you must remember how chaotic everything was at that time. There were literally millions of displaced people, many of whom lacked any identification papers at all, or any way of establishing their credentials. It was, unfortunately, an open invitation for the unscrupulous and the desperate to take advantage of the goodwill of those trying to sort out the mess.'

Clemency tried to look interested. Two days of travelling and Pryce-Jones's urbane tones were starting to weigh down her eyelids.

'That's how it was that a number of former Nazis

were able to enter Argentina in the years after the war. Mostly they were small fry, but there were a few like Eichmann who were more senior. Three of those are now of particular interest to us: Walter Ullmann, Reinhard Werner and Dr Adolf Zoll. This sheet has their background information – height, place of birth, distinguishing marks and so on. You'll need to memorize it all and give the sheet back to Mr Linklater this evening. As far as possible, you should refer to them by their code names. Ullmann is Faith, Werner is Hope and Zoll is Charity.'

Pryce-Jones looked at his watch.

'I think we're done here,' he said.

'What should I do when I'm not in these archives?'

'Do?' Pryce-Jones stared. 'I suggest you sleep.'

'Maybe a little bit of sight-seeing would be more in character,' Hal suggested. 'It would look a bit odd if she took all her meals in her room.'

'Very well. But remember, Miss White, you're not here to enjoy yourself. You have one task to complete, and then we can send you back to London. Please don't let some tango dancer sweep you off your feet. That seems to be all the rage amongst the Embassy clerks.'

Delivered with a cold smile, this pleasantry hurt like a slap on the cheek.

'I wouldn't do that,' she said; but he was already letting himself out. Hal raised an eyebrow as he passed her – almost a kind of solidarity.

'Until this evening… darling.'

2

The phone rang a little before ten o'clock. Clemency had been up for an hour, eaten some sandwiches and coffee in her room, and had a shower to try and stay awake.

'I'll be across the street. Dark blue Triumph. All ready?'

'Yes, but what should I wear?'

She could hear him chuckle and knew he was thinking *just like a girl*.

'Something you don't mind getting dusty,' he said, and rang off.

She'd put on a tweed skirt and a plain black cotton sweater. That would do as well as anything. She took a last look at the descriptions of Ullmann, Werner and Zoll and then took the lift down to the lobby where she dropped off her key.

They drove off in silence. She was surprised by the affluence on show in the shops, their windows bright in the night. It might have been any European city, except for the people strolling about at such a late hour, just like Madrid. But despite the bustle of the streets, it had a melancholic feel.

'Tell me about Faith,' Hal asked.

'Height one metre eighty-two. Brown eyes, dark brown hair. Age 52. Born Leipzig 22 October 1912. Married Elli Forsach in 1938. Two children, Hermann and Horst, born in 1939 and 1941. Last known posting was to the regional Luftwaffe command in upper Austria.'

'Very good. How old is Zoll?'

'62.'

'Where did Hope study chemistry.'

'He didn't. He studied engineering in Munich.'

'Excellent. The crib?'

She took the sheet from her handbag and passed it to him.

'Made a copy? Or any notes?'

'No.'

'There are matches in the glovebox. Set fire to it. Make sure it's all gone.'

She did as she was told, grinding the ashes into the carpet in the footwell. They came to a large square, lined with grand buildings, all classical porticos and Baroque domes.

'I'm sorry about the mix-up over what you're here to do,' he said. 'In a way, I should admire your enthusiasm. Or maybe you didn't know what it was you'd have been getting into. Going after killers is always going to be a bit dicey. Like hunting man-eating tigers. You have to get them before they get you.'

'I suppose so.'

He cut across two lanes at the junction and turned into a diagonal street just ahead of a taxi.

'Have you been here long?' she asked. 'You seem to know it well.'

'A week. But I have a wonderful sense of direction.'

'Why these three?' she said. 'Ullmann, Werner and Zoll?'

'I can't tell you.'

'I thought maybe they'd done something particularly bad.'

'You'd have to ask Pryce-Jones.'

'I'm not just being nosy. If I'm looking through all these files, there may be something relevant. I'll miss it if I don't know what I'm looking for.'

'Ordinarily, I'd agree. But on this one it's vital that you only know the immediate facts. It's for your own protection.'

'Really?'

'Look, this country has a very large German community. It also has a lot of people at the top – the very top – who are quite happy with having former Nazis living here. There are people who would cheerfully snatch you off the street and interrogate you if they found out what we were up to. So it's important that you know nothing. You see?'

'I suppose so.' By 'interrogate', she guessed Hal meant 'torture'. If that happened to her, would having nothing to say really help? What he really wanted to protect was the mission. She could accept that. She just wished he would be honest about it.

By now they had left the shops and apartment blocks behind, with a high wall on one side and a row of warehouses on the other. There was no other traffic and the lights showed nothing moving except a stray dog nosing around a bin.

They stopped by the entrance to an alley. Around them was silence, though they could still hear the city, like a distant waterfall. There was also a freshness in the air that showed they were near the river.

'We're a bit conspicuous here,' Hal said quietly. 'If anyone comes, I'll grab you and we'll pretend to be lovers.'

'Will we?' she replied dryly.

'Have you a better idea?'

He didn't wait for a response, but set off down the alley towards the back of a long, two-story warehouse made of brick. There were no windows, except for a clerestory set into the tiled roof. The single door was smooth to the wall, with no handle, and clearly barred from the inside.

They moved along the side of the building, but there was no obvious way in. At the far end, the way was blocked by a tall wall, topped with spikes. Clemency looked at it dubiously. If she could get onto the roof, she was sure she could prise one of the windows open. But the brickwork was old and crumbling, and she hated the idea of trusting to it, poised above those spikes.

'What's the plan, then?' Hal asked.

She paced slowly back along the side of the building, saying nothing, hoping it looked like she was making an intelligent assessment of the options, rather than simply buying time. But it wasn't so long ago that she'd been climbing in and out of her boarding school at night. This wasn't much more difficult. At intervals, there were drain-pipes, and if she sacrificed her scarf, something might be possible.

She examined the pipes more carefully. They were cast iron, pitted with rust but still solid, though the fittings that kept them to the wall gave her some anxiety. But there was no time for doubts. She wrapped the scarf around her and slipped the two ends between the pipe and the wall and knotted them together. Then she kicked off her shoes and pulled herself up, bracing her feet against the wall and leaning back so that the scarf was taut against the pipe. She'd only seen this done before by the men who installed telephone lines, but to her surprise it worked.

Soon she was ten feet off the ground, her knees

beginning to ache, but confident she could make the top.

'I'll need some time inside,' she called down softly. 'At least an hour.'

'Remember, if you're caught, you're nothing to do with us.'

She climbed on, filled with fury. Peter would never have behaved like this, whatever his orders. He'd have found a way to get her out, just as he had gone over the Czech border to rescue his agent Stanêk. But Hal didn't matter. She was doing this for Peter. One day, he would come back, and they would be together, and then they would...

Before she knew it, she had reached the line of the roof and was hitching up her skirt and half-rolling onto the tiles. She lay on her back, catching her breath and looking up at the night sky, glowing faintly with the lights from the docks and the city. In her mind, she was making a list of equipment she would need when she returned. Gloves. Rope. A set of picks, in case there were locks to open inside.

She edged her way up the roof to the base of the clerestory. The windows were filthy, and it was impossible to see anything inside, but they only had a simple catch which she soon had open. She stuck her head in, but it was as black as a well and she was loath to use her torch. She thought she could make out a darker patch beneath her that might be the top of a line of shelves. But it was hard to judge distances. Was it two feet down, or twenty?

She wriggled through the gap and let her feet slide down, her toes reaching out for some purchase.

Nothing.

Her legs kicking in emptiness, she lowered herself

further, trusting she would have the strength to pull herself up again. Then her toes brushed against a ledge. She explored, until she had an impression of the top of a massive wooden structure, surely solid enough to bear her weight. She let go, crouching down.

For a long time she waited, letting her senses explore the building. It was a trick she'd learned in the woods around her home in Dorset; how to stay still and quiet, until you no longer felt like an intruder, but part of the night, with the same right to be there as the badgers and foxes she'd come to watch. At last she began to make sense of the faint light and deep shadows. The place was at least two stories tall, as wide as a church, with a gallery running along both walls. Everywhere there were cabinets and shelves, each weighed with the accumulated paper of decades.

She climbed down to the gallery, realising how far she was from home, in this half-derelict warehouse in an unknown city. Yet she felt quite safe. The warm, dry smell of the paper was familiar, comforting, as was the knowledge that no-one really cared about what was stored here, and there was little chance of her being discovered. At heart, this was her place, just as if she were back in the chancery in the Embassy in Bern, pulling a file or checking a cross-reference.

She ran her hand over one of the cabinets. These were not the steel she was used to but solid varnished wood. She eased a draw out and felt the masses of paper inside, folder after folder, perhaps a hundred in the one drawer, and each cabinet had four drawers, and there might be a hundred or more cabinets along the wall, the same on the far side, and more in rows down the centre. Opening folders at random, there were forms, carbon copies, documents, curling passport photos, the faces masks of hope and fear. It was like a cathedral to paper; each file a prayer for a new start away from the poverty, the violence and the hatred of Europe. They had come to Argentina for a new and better life: so many victims of persecution; and amongst them, without shame, were hidden some of their persecutors. So many sheep; and also the wolves.

The landing cards were on the nearest of the galleries. She climbed back up the iron stairs, her hand following the rail, her feet feeling in the darkness. She opened one of the drawers almost at random and pulled out a handful of cards. They were printed forms, about ten inches by six, filled in with faded handwriting. At times it was hard to make out the words. Again, each had a photograph in one corner, held in place by a rusted staple. All of them looked like criminals; even the women; even the children.

Each card had a serial number that appeared to match the date of issue. She was in April 1953. She put the cards back and walked along the gallery, using the torch cautiously to illuminate the dates written on the front of each drawer. 1952... 1951...

There were more than three hundred cards in each drawer, and literally hundreds of drawers. Her heart sank at the thought of how long it would take her to read through the cards, decipher the names, let alone see if she could match one to Ullmann, Werner or Zoll.

It was typical of someone like Pryce-Jones. He would never have filed a piece of paper in his life. There were people like Clemency to do it for him. Still, she could hardly complain, or ask to give it up and go home. She was there to do a job. Proving herself to Swan was worth any amount of Hal's flirting and Pryce-Jones' condescension.

There was also, she had to admit, the lure of this unknown country – that same feeling she'd had on arriving in the hotel that morning. Argentina was a blank page, except for the tango. Maybe there was somewhere she could learn the steps.

If only Peter were here too…

She pulled out the first draw of January 1946 and began to work her way through. Occasionally a particularly puzzling or badly-scrawled name would hold her up, but she soon settled into a rhythm, getting through the cards a little faster.

Time passed. She worked on, occasionally stopping to stretch, or rest her eyes. She wished she had a flask of coffee to keep her going.

Then, from far off, a church bell rang. One o'clock. She had been working for over an hour and had reached the fourth of January. With a sick feeling, she worked out how long the job would take, and realised it was not even weeks, more like months. It was so preposterous that she wondered if it were deliberate. She had forced Swan to give her this chance to prove her worth. Had he chosen this mission for her, knowing it was impossible?

She forced herself to think. All she was interested in were those who were entering Argentina for the first time and had a visa allowing permanent residency. These were perhaps only one in twenty. If she only checked those, not the rest, it would still be days of work; but no longer weeks. She began to flick through the cards, picking out the ones marked resident visa, pausing only when something in the photograph or the description could possibly be matched to one of her targets.

She soon reached the 5th of January, and in some

further recess of her mind, another cog clicked on. These cards recorded the serial numbers of the visa. Which meant that somewhere there must be a file that contained the original visa application. If you could find those, there would be no need to scan hundreds of thousands of landing cards. You could simply look at the applications for residency permits. Ten or twenty thousand at most.

Where would you keep those files? Surely somewhere in this very building.

She closed the drawer and conjured up an image of these files in her mind. Much larger than a landing card. The kind that were passed from office to office, signed off at each stage. A cardboard cover. Foolscap. You'd need a proper filing cabinet to hold them. Like the cabinets on the ground floor.

After a few minutes reading labels and poking about, she found what she wanted.

They were filed by year, but – and when she found this out she did a kind of dance of pure joy – each year was in alphabetical order.

Five minutes later, she was holding the visa application for Reinhard Werner.

3

They drove through the quiet of the city to an all-night café in one of the *barrios* on the south side, busy with workers from the nearby meat-packing plants. Over coffee and little custard pastries Clemency revealed what she had learned.

'There's no record of Faith or Charity being granted an entry visa between 1945 and 1960. So if they came here, it was under an assumed name.'

'And Werner?' Hal asked, not bothering with the codenames.

She couldn't suppress her triumph any longer.

'I found him. He applied for a visa through the Argentinian embassy in Rome in April 1947. It was granted three months later. He travelled out from Genoa on the *SS Vicenza* and landed on the 17th October.'

She passed on a scrap of paper recording all the information, plus the names and addresses of the Argentinian citizens who had sponsored him and the address where he intended to stay. Hal was impressed: not as much as he should have been, but still definitely pleased.

'Good show. We'll pop you back in there tonight and you can keep digging. Now we'd better get you back to your hotel.'

They drove in silence, Hal turning something over in his mind. Clemency felt herself drifting off to sleep.

'I need you to pick up some papers this afternoon,' he said abruptly. 'I would go but there's a lot on.'

Inwardly, she sighed. She'd been counting on sleeping for a few hours, and then exploring the city. But at least she wouldn't be confined to her hotel room.

'There's a lawyer called Cristina Navarra. She approached the Embassy a few months back saying she had some evidence about Nazi war criminals living in Argentina. I don't think much will come of it but if you could pick up what she's got, it would save me a chore.'

'Will I need to speak to her?'

'No, but if you do, just say you're a clerk at the Embassy. Temporary cover for a few weeks. Something like that. After that, just play dumb.'

'I can do that,' she said, but he didn't seem to notice her sarcasm.

'Leave the papers with Pryce-Jones. I'll pick you up this evening. Same as before.'

◊

Clemency awoke ravenously hungry and soon to be disappointed by what passed for breakfast. She then set out to buy the equipment she needed, finding most of it at an ironmongers and extending her Spanish vocabulary in unexpected ways. The sun rose higher, penetrating the canyons formed by the apartment blocks along the streets, and the city shed some of the melancholy of the night before. There were trees along the wide avenues, and cafes where men and women sat reading or chatting or watching their fellow citizens stroll by. There were elegant lamp-posts, and the streets were clean and when she saw two policemen pass on the other side of the street, they were not at all threatening; no sinister moustaches or tinted sunglasses. It could have been a European city – not Paris, it didn't take itself seriously enough for that, but perhaps Milan or Barcelona.

She strolled at random until she came across a bookshop and bought a city guide. The lawyer's office was in the north, a district called Recolta, and Clemency had a couple of spare hours when she could play at being a tourist.

She had lunch at Constitución, one of the main line stations. A station buffet was less conspicuous for a woman eating alone, and she had already learned that men were ready to call out to her in the street, look her over, even try and touch her. All that wasn't unknown in London, or even in Bern, but here it was elevated to an art form.

She also felt very obviously not Argentinian, particularly when she ventured onto the underground railway that they called *El Subte*. There was the same mix of familiar and exotic that she felt everywhere in the city. If she shut her eyes, the smell of burnt dust and hot oil took her back to the London Underground, and the roof over the platform was arched just like in the Paris *Métro*, but nothing was really the same. No doubt the passengers in the gloom of the ill-lit train could sense the same in her.

By now the heat and her tiredness were catching up with her and she was grateful when her route took her past a cemetery open to the public, where she could stroll or sit quietly until it was time to see the lawyer. But even here the sun was remorseless, and there were few trees and little shade. Argentinians, it seemed, liked to spend their money on vast and tasteless tombs, more

like small houses than graves, and these were crammed
in along the narrow paths like books on a bookshelf.
Each competed with the other for attention, to promote
the family name of those lying dead inside, with domes
and pillars, statues and inscriptions. She felt suddenly
homesick, thinking of the churchyard next to her family
home, with its quiet weathered stones and rough lawns
and the long shadows of the yew trees.

It soon struck her how varied the surnames on each
tomb were, and how few were Spanish. There were
Italians, Poles, French and English, Scandinavian and
Russian and German. Spanish might be the language
of the country, but the roots of its people led back
to every corner of Europe and beyond. Was this one
reason why the Nazi fugitives had not been treated
with more suspicion, in a city that was inhabited only
by immigrants?

The massive tombs and the narrow passages soon
felt oppressive. She wouldn't have wanted to wander
alone here at night. Anyway, it was time to pick up the
papers.

She was soon entering the cool lobby of an Art Deco
office block. Navarra's firm was on the ninth floor, and
she took the lift, already planning her fastest route back
to the hotel and her bed. But when she explained why
she was there to the impossibly glamorous receptionist,
she was asked to wait.

Clemency picked up a newspaper, but the news was
about politicians she didn't know and controversies
she didn't understand, like coming into a conversation
half-way through. The secretary, having brought
Clemency a cup of mint tea, was busy with her typing.
Clemency wondered for the first time about Navarra.
There were few enough female lawyers in England, let

alone in a country like Argentina, where the position of women seemed much more traditional. Yet Navarra was a partner here, and the place seemed prosperous.

At last, the secretary rose and led Clemency down the corridor. No-one had come out of any of the offices, so Navarra wasn't in a meeting with anyone, and Clemency guessed she had been kept waiting for a reason.

Cristina Navarra was in her forties, her thick dark hair cut in a fringe that almost covered her eyes and fell to her shoulders like a mane. She came forward to shake Clemency's hand, very business-like, then waved her to a chair and returned to her desk, moving with the strength and grace of a jaguar. It was soon clear she had something of the same fierce temperament.

'So Señor Linklater was unable to come.'

Clemency tried to explain, but this was waved away.

'He would like you to take away the papers?'

'Yes.'

'But I was to discuss these papers with Señor Linklater before giving them to him. It is most important that they are used in the correct way. And he is not here...'

She raised her hands in frustration. Clemency, having nothing useful to say, sat quietly. Navarra wore a linen suit in jungle green that brought out the olive tones of her skin and was almost military in its cut. Like a guerrilla leader, Clemency thought, like the women who had fought for Castro in Cuba, descending from the mountains and cutting the throats of their enemies.

'You are with the Embassy?' Navarra asked. 'You understand the work Señor Linklater is doing?'

'Oh, yes.'

Her angry eyes rested on Clemency a little longer, and then she made up her mind.

'I can only give you these papers if I believe that my client would wish it. This depends on what you plan to do with them. Can you tell me that?'

'No. I don't know.'

'And Señor Linklater is not here. I ask myself, can I trust him?'

'You can trust me,' Clemency said impulsively, feeling this was all slipping away.

'You?' Navarra tipped her head to one side. Then she smiled faintly, as if appreciating for the first time the bind that Clemency was in.

'Very well. I will explain to you and then you can explain to the elusive Señor Linklater. Have you lived here in Argentina for long?'

'No, this is my first day.'

'Truly? Then we may need a little more time.' She leaned forward to the intercom on her desk and ordered tea. Then she rested one hand on a thick envelope that lay on her desk. These would be the documents that Clemency had come for.

'In Argentina, we are a country of immigrants,' Navarra began. 'Most came only for a better life. They worked hard, they raised their families. But not all. Some were criminals, Fascists, murderers. They came here to escape justice.'

'After the war in Europe, things in my country were difficult. You have heard of Perón? Yes? I am not one of those who think he is a god, and nor was he a devil. But he did some bad things. One was to send to Europe to seek out these criminals, because they were useful to him. He dreamed of our being the great power in Latin America. He brought men here who could build tanks and jet planes. He encouraged them to set up factories for chemicals and medicines.

If they had money, so much the better, and he did not ask where that money came from.'

By now Cristina was on her feet, pacing about restlessly, one hand moving like a conductor's to draw out the thread of her thoughts.

'But these men who came, they brought something else. Like an illness, a virus, they brought their politics, their beliefs. They hated the Communists, and the Jews, and the Socialists. They believed in power, and they despised democracy. Because they were rich, and worked hard, and joined together in a kind of brotherhood, they have become very, very powerful in my country. They influence the politicians, the judges, the chiefs of police. It is not always money, you understand. There are gifts to the charities that are most valued, or contributions to the campaigns of the politicians. But now they are stronger perhaps than those who want democracy to flourish. This is of great concern to many people here. Including my client.'

'More than the crimes they committed?'

'One follows the other. While they are powerful, we cannot bring justice. Look at the case of Eichmann. There are a thousand more protected in the same way.'

'But don't we want the same thing?'

'Yes, but you, and your Señor Linklater, do you understand my country? We have all come here from elsewhere, different religions, different races, even. There is one thing that we all believe in, and that is Argentina. Patriotism, pride in our country, it is at the heart of everything. This is the weapon that these men use. Provoke them, and they have a card to play that is stronger than anything in our hand. They point to the Jews, and they say, the Jews are working against us. They are undermining our country. They are not loyal

to Argentina, but to themselves, or to Israel. When
Eichmann was taken, the people of my country, we
did not say, this is a great day for justice. We did not
ask, who were the men who allowed him to stay, and
who protected him? We said, this is an insult to our
sovereignty.'

She sat on the edge of her desk, leaning forward,
intent on Clemency understanding.

'You know what they did? They spat at Jews in the
street. They broke windows. They took a Jewish girl
and they cut her here and here,' she said, gesturing at
her cheeks. 'All to show who the real enemy were. Not
the Fascists, but the Jews. And because they are in the
government, and they own the newspapers, they can
make us believe it. You see?'

Clemency hardly dared do anything else but agree.

'Capturing Eichmann was good for Israel, and for
justice, but not so good for Argentina. We need to deal
with these men in our own way, through the law, and
with evidence. Is this what Señor Linklater wants? Or
does he want to show that the British have clean hands,
while those of Argentina are dirty? You see now why
I do not want to hand over this information to him,
without talking to him first?'

'Yes.'

She nodded, seemingly satisfied, then slid off the
desk and went to the window. It was as if she wanted
to escape from the office and hunt down these men
herself.

'Please understand, if I am angry, it is not with you.
Only I wish to be understood.'

'I'll tell Mr Linklater,' Clemency reassured her,
standing up. But Navarra, having delivered her
impassioned speech, seemed inclined to chat.

'How long are you to stay in Buenos Aires?'

'Not long. A week or two, maybe.'

'Truly? Then you must see and do everything before you go. What are your plans?'

'I don't really have any.'

'Do not waste your time going where the Embassy people go. You must be a *porteña*, if only for a few weeks. You must go to the theatre – your Spanish is excellent – and cafés, and go riding at the weekend. And tango, of course. You dance?'

'Not the tango.'

'Then you must learn. My friend Lucia, she will teach you. This is her job, you understand.' She wrote quickly on a notepad and tore the page off to give to Clemency. 'She will not charge you. In this city, everything is favours. I prepare the lease of her apartment, she shows you our national dance, so you will understand us, and we can work together. You see?'

In this friendly mood, Cristina Navarra was still quite alarming, but Clemency took the paper.

'Thank you.'

'I will call her. She will expect you tomorrow. And by then, perhaps Señor Linklater will find the time to see me.'

'I'm sure he will.'

4

Hal collected her from the hotel at ten o'clock and once again they drove thorough the city towards the docks. Clemency had worried tabout returning without the papers, but he appeared to have lost interest in them. This was disconcerting, when she thought of the passion with which Cristina had spoken about the Nazi emigrés in her country. But if he were missing a trick, it wasn't her place to say so.

They parked near the alley and waited for a few minutes in case there was anyone about. She showed him the light nylon rope and the rest of the equipment that she had bought that morning and that would make climbing into the archive much easier. He listened politely, but she suspected he was amused rather than impressed.

A car came along the road. Hal pulled her to him and began to kiss her, holding her painfully tight when she tried to pull away.

'Come on,' he said. 'Look like you're enjoying it.'

She leaned closer as if to nibble at his neck, which was a lot better than kissing him on the lips. The lights from the passing car lit them up and his hand strayed down to cup her breast.

'If I slap you,' she whispered, 'that could look realistic.'

'You'll find I'm irresistible,' he replied. But his hand

went no further. And once the red lights of the car had faded away, he let her go.

'Much as I'd love to do that again...'

'I'll see you back here at four,' she replied, her voice choked with fury. She got out of the car, and he raised his hand in salute and sped off. She stood for a moment, still sensing where he had touched her, and the taste of his aftershave acrid on her tongue. Her face was burning and she was grateful for the cool night air, damp from the nearby river.

It took her only a few minutes to scale the wall and let herself down into the archive. She soon settled into a rhythm. The time passed quickly, and she was surprised when the chimes of a distant church told her she had been there for almost two hours. She turned up a couple of possible leads for Ullmann, though nothing for Zoll, and decided to reward herself with some coffee. Finding a Thermos had been the high point of her morning and the hotel had obligingly filled it. She drank it gratefully and ate some squares of chocolate.

The door below her crashed open. She barely had time to switch off her torch before there were footsteps below her, two pairs of heavy boots striding confidently down the main aisle. The beam of a flashlight began to play over the rows of cabinets, and the two guards continued their conversation, far too colloquial for her to understand.

She shrank back into the shadows, hoping they wouldn't bother coming up the stairs to the upper galleries.

She risked a glance down and her heart sank. They were young, swaggering along very conscious of their uniforms and their status, the guns and batons on their belts. She was thankful for her dark clothes, but wished she had a mask.

The men were exchanging anecdotes, and she realised it was something about a woman, perhaps a prostitute, and something in their tone made her go cold. Some of the young men on the street had been predatory enough, despite being in the open and in daylight. What if these two found her? Alone, at night, two against one?

Now there were boots on the iron staircase up to the gallery. She pressed herself against the base of the nearest cabinet, hoping to blend in with the shadows. Dust tickled her nose, and she held her breath. If the man came along, he would almost need to step over her. Then he would pull her to her feet, and she imagined the slow, greedy smile, the shout down to his companion, his hands pulling her out into the light.

She wished he had a knife. The self-defence she had been taught wouldn't be enough to deal with both of them. And if she fought, then once they had subdued her, their blood would be up and the rest would follow.

He reached the top of the stairs. She could feel the beam of his torch running down the length of the gallery, gently playing over her. A horrible moment of silence, as if the man was trying to puzzle out the curious shape. Then more footsteps, but these were going down, and the men were talking again, walking back towards the entrance.

She breathed out.

Too soon. They stopped. She could almost hear one of the men looking around.

'*¿Hueles café?*

Even with his accent, she could understand: *can you smell coffee?*

After a moment, the other man laughed, and they were moving. The door crashed shut behind them, and silence returned.

◊

An hour later, and she was safe in Hal's car. He was pleased with what she had found, but showed no contrition for having misled her about the lack of security.

'It only goes to prove what I said,' he said, speeding though the empty streets. 'The less you know, the better.'

He was right, of course. But that didn't stop Clemency hating him for saying it.

'Anyway, you can have a good old rest before tonight.'

Perhaps it was a compliment, his assumption she would go back to the archive, despite the extra risk. And he was right. She had been so frightened by the prospect of being caught, and what they might do to her. But that was as nothing compared to the exhilaration of escaping them. It was like a drug, and she could still feel it sweeping through her veins, making her muscles twitch. It would be hard to sleep.

At least the afternoon would bring some distraction.

◊

The address was a bar on Avenida Soler, all warm, dark-stained mahogany, nicotine-cream walls and high frosted windows. It was shut, empty except for a young man in a white singlet. He let her in and told her to wait: or at least, Clemency assumed so, for she still wasn't used to the sibilant *Porteño* accent. There were little wooden tables and chairs around the sides, leaving a central space for dancing. The walls were lined with framed photographs of men in dramatic poses, smouldering women, none of whom meant anything to Clemency. After a few moments, a woman dressed all in black, tall and with dramatic dark eyes, came through a door at the far end and held out her hand.

'I am Lucia Sabatini. Welcome.'

She spoke with the mix of formality and theatricality that Clemency was coming to think of as the Argentinian way. She was also determined to establish her authority from the start, sending Clemency to change and criticising her shoes. She explained the basic moves, and they looked straightforward enough to Clemency, who thought of herself as a fairly good dancer.

Then Lucia put on a record, a soulful lament with the distinctive rhythms in accordion and violin, and they began. It reminded Clemency of the dancing lessons at school, with a strict teacher and having to stand up with another girl, each taking turns to lead. But in Lucia's iron grip, and with a constant stream of comments and commands – *bend, forward, two-three and again* – she thought she'd done pretty well by the time the record came to an end.

'How was I?' she asked.

'Awful. Awful awful awful. Of what are you thinking when you dance? Something you must buy from a shop? A book you are reading? What?'

'I'm sorry.' But this only infuriated Lucia further.

'Sorry? You are the woman that I would throw my life away for you, and you tell me you are sorry? Do you not know what Tango is about? You must listen to the music. You must feel the movement. You must think to yourself that you are a most beautiful woman, and the man who is dancing with you, if you wished he would fall at your feet, marry you, sleep with you, die for you, because you are so beautiful. You see? And maybe you will choose him. Maybe he is the man for you. The dance, it is the way to find out. Does he care for you? Does he think of you? Are his eyes on you or is he looking to see who he wants to dance with next?'

Clemency smiled.

'It is true,' Lucia insisted, 'Then, maybe you stick a knife in him. Or maybe you dance with all your passion, so that he forgets every other woman in the world.'

'You make it sound like a cheap thriller.'

'Of course. It is the drama of life. That is what you dance. But you English, maybe it is true what they say, that inside here,' – he laid his palm on Clemency's chest – 'there is nothing. No heart. No feeling. Is this so?'

'Of course not.'

'Then show it to me. Come.'

For all her harsh words, she guided Clemency back onto the floor with perfect civility. This must just be her style, and she had thawed a bit by the time the hour was up.

'Is this same time on Thursday good for you?' Lucia asked. Clemency began to explain that it might be difficult for her to afford private lessons, but Lucia brushed that aside.

'I said to Cristina that I would teach you. A favour, of course. I expect you have done something of value for her.'

'Not really.'

'Then maybe she has plans for you.'

◊

She returned to the hotel in a hurry, only to find Hal
in her room, waiting for her. As before, he was very
much at home, reading the *Herald*, the city's main
English-language newspaper, and smoking a cigarette.

'Your plans for tonight have changed,' he said.
'You'd better put your best frock on. We're going to
the *Bavaria*.'

'What's that?'

'One of the oldest clubs in Buenos Aires. Much
frequented by the German community. I'm developing
my character of the rich young man who's fed up with
the way that England is turning into a meritocracy.
Occasionally I throw in a comment about international
Jewry. With a little luck, someone will let their guard
down.'

'Are we going there now?'

'No, the Embassy first. Catsmeat wants a word.'

'Why? What have I done?'

'Yes, it is a bit like being summoned to see the
headmaster, isn't it? The thing is, London have let
us down slightly. They told us they had a girl to send
out to work with me on the trip up to Misiones, but
apparently that's fallen through. Given that you were
so keen to go in the first place...'

She was delighted; but she didn't show it. It would
do him good to eat some of his words.

'Don't you need a trained agent?' she asked sweetly.

'Well, obviously that would be preferable.'

'Or maybe it's something that could be done by any

half-competent secretary or clerk?'

He had the grace to wince.

'Hardly. But I wasn't joking about the risk. If our cover's blown, it could get awkward.'

'And is Mr Pryce-Jones happy with this?'

'I wouldn't say exactly happy.'

'Perhaps in his mind one woman will be just as good, or bad, as another.'

'Something like that,' he replied with a smile. 'So you're in?'

'Well, yes, but what about my cover? And how long are we going for?'

'Let's talk about that after you've seen Catsmeat.'

Half an hour later they passed the British Embassy, flag hanging limp in the still warm air, and parked a little further down the road. The voice of the guard on the gate – pure sergeant-major – made her nostalgic not only for England but for her own Embassy in Bern, where Corson would have come out to see the visitors in just the same way, greeting them politely but with no trace of servility.

Hal seemed to know his way about, leading Clemency upstairs, past a series of framed etchings of London parks of surprising dullness.

'Pryce-Jones is the third door along. I'm going to sort out a telegram but I'll join you later. Don't worry,' he added, seeing Clemency's hesitation. 'He's perfectly harmless.'

Second time around, Pryce-Jones was more civil, in his old-fashioned, mannered way – she didn't think anyone had ever called her 'My dear lady' before – and asked how she was enjoying the city. When she mentioned her tango lesson with Lucia, he became surprisingly positive, insisting she must make time for this and tell him how she was getting on.

Then, his social duty done, he handed her a new British passport made out in the name of Caroline Black, but from which her own face stared out. She discovered she had been born in Cheltenham, was 5' 8" tall and had brown eyes and brown hair, and was a spinster. Apart from being told that she was to take her orders from Hal for the rest of the mission, it seems that this was all the briefing she needed.

'One other thing,' he said. 'I spoke to my wife about what you might need by way of clothes and luggage and so on. She also said for me to tell you that if you wanted any advice about the best shops to go to, you had only to ask.'

He then handed to her a fat envelope of pesos with the air of a man for whom such sums were of little consequence. A wealthy background wasn't uncommon in the Foreign Office. Bright young grammar school boys from Leeds or Liverpool might be making their way in the theatre, or television, and might even turn up in the Treasury, but definitely not in the Office. A classical education, polish and connections to the right people – the kind with lands and titles and a deep-rooted stake in the country – were still what was expected.

She counted the cash surreptitiously on the stairs. It was more than enough to play the part of a rich man's fiancée. Spending it would be fun.

Hal was waiting outside, chatting to the guard.

'Ah, Miss Black. Shall we go?'

'What do I need to know about you?' she asked, as they walked towards the car. He now made a point of opening the door for her, as a fiancé should.

'My wife must never criticise my driving, my

drinking or my gambling. Am I to call you Clemency or Caroline?'

'It says Caroline on my passport,' she replied. 'But you should do whatever you think is right. I know absolutely nothing about any of this.'

'How's your Spanish coming on?'

'It's good enough. The accent here is different.'

'What gun do you usually carry?'

'Gun? I don't have one.'

'Have you ever used one?'

For Clemency, these brittle, knowing exchanges suddenly turned sour.

'Yes, I have.'

'Well, it shouldn't come to anything like that, but I'll see what the Embassy can arrange. At least you won't be precious about the calibre or the grip. People can be so funny.'

'If you think I need one then by all means let me have it. But generally I'm not precious about anything.'

'That's good. We're going to be working rather closely over the next few weeks. Although maybe the odd flaming row would be good for our cover.'

They sped off. Hal began a lecture.

'This mess-up with London – I say mess-up, though I'm beginning to think Swan always meant you to be the one we ended up with, and this other girl agent was just an invention – is a bit of a problem, because we don't have much time to rehearse our roles. The thing to hold on to is that no-one is going to suspect that we're not who we say we are, unless we give them good reason. So, for example, someone will ask you when you got here and how your flight was. It doesn't really matter what you say, because they aren't really interested. It's just passing the time. Whatever you say, do it with confidence. If they do start to look suspicious, just say you must have misunderstood what they were asking – but then, just make it look like you don't care what they think, one way or another. Right?'

'Right.'

'Never apologise, never explain. It's not a bad lesson for life. Make it your motto when you're working undercover. Also, we can anticipate pretty much every question we'll be asked. Where did we meet? When are we getting married? That sort of thing. We can hammer all that out over dinner. In fact, here we are.'

He pulled up outside a restaurant and soon they were being escorted to a table by the manager, and followed by the *sommelier* with his oversized wine list, while lesser beings pulled out chairs for them and flicked their napkins into their laps. Looking about at the glamour and wealth on display, Clemency felt quite dowdy.

'It won't always be like this,' Hal said, for once suggesting he had some understanding of what she was thinking. 'In a couple of days we'll be up-country. It'll be much easier to fit in. You won't be worried about not being festooned in diamonds and pearls.'

'That will be a relief. How do we get there?'

'We'll drive. I'm having a few adjustments made to the car tomorrow, and then we can be off on Friday.' He stopped as the head waiter approached. 'Is there anything you don't eat?'

She assured him there wasn't, without realising he planned to order for her.

'We'll start with a dozen each of the oysters *a la malvinas*. Then the Señorita will have the salmon *en croute* with the *epinards*. and I shall have the *tournedos*, very rare, dusted in salt and pepper, with *frites, sauce bearnaise* and a tossed green salad. The oil is first pressing virgin olive, I trust?'

'But of course, Señor.'

The steak sounded delicious and she hoped Hal might slide her a piece in exchange for some of her salmon; but when she looked around at the starched white linen, the discreet lighting and the way the staff held their noses slightly in the air, she knew that swaps were not possible.

He took the same approach to the wine, showing far more interest in the opinion of the *sommelier* than in what she might like. Then again, she'd only found out the day before that they made wine in Argentina, so she would have had little to add.

She'd been taken out to dinner many times, but no-one had ever ordered for her before like this. Was it gallant? Presumptuous? Either way, she'd have to go along with it. Beneath the fiction that they were in love, she was her boss, her commanding officer, and if they started to argue, it would put the mission in danger. Peter had always told her she had to learn to obey without question. She was there only because of Peter; because of her deal with Swan. She could up with a hundred snide remarks, a hundred more moments of unwanted attention, if it would bring Peter a day closer to freedom.

5

The *Club Bavaria* was in a quiet street of substantial
villas standing back from the road behind high walls
and ornate ironwork. There were lawns shaded
by some kind of pine trees, light spilling from the
windows, and a genial noise of chatter and music.
Clemency was greeted deferentially by a doorman
and relieved of her coat. Then they passed into a
brightly-lit salon filled with people, all talking loudly,
half-drowning the string quartet playing Strauss at the
far end. There were broad backs in dark cloth, and
swelling stomachs; much bare shoulder and glittering
jewellery, high brittle laughter and self-satisfied
puffing on cigars.

Clemency stood in the doorway, as if on the edge
of a high diving-board, gathering herself to make the
plunge into this pool of wealthy confidence. Then Hal
had her arm and was leading her forward, apparently
completely at home. Before she could draw breath,
she was being introduced to people, accepting a drink
from a blank-faced waiter, drawn into chit-chat about
the latest Cary Grant movie. Slowly she began to read
the scene and understand the German-ness of it. The
men and women around her were much like those at
the Embassy parties in Bern. The wine was sweeter
than she would have chosen, but it could have come
from the banks of the Moselle.

Her job was to be at Hal's side, playing her part, looking at him adoringly as he chatted on, occasionally saying something light and uncontroversial of her own. It was dull, and there was no prospect of dancing – the only thing that made this kind of gathering bearable. When Hal said something about it being time for cards, she went in search of coffee.

The buffet was laid out on a long table, and Clemency made her way past plates of sliced meats, arrays of smoked sausages in ringed patterns, bowls of potato salad, of *sauerkraut*, of pickles, baskets of dark bread, ramekins of mustard, until she reached the desserts.

'Sometimes I wish for just some soup.'

The woman who'd spoken was about her own age, but taller, with blond hair piled in a chignon. She wasn't looking at Clemency, but it was an introduction of a kind.

'It all looks lovely,' Clemency ventured.

'The *lebkuchen* will be good,' her new friend said. 'The baker is from Munich.'

Obediently, Clemency picked up the tongs and placed a piece onto her plate.

'So you are English.'

It was a statement, but also a question.

'Yes. My fiancé is buying a farm here.'

'Cattle?'

Typically, the first question she had to answer was one she had not discussed with Hal.

'I think so. I don't know much about farming. I leave that to Hal.'

'Then he must speak to my father. He has a business that exports meat. My name is Petra Rausch,' she added, extending her hand.

'Caroline Black,' Clemency replied, recalling her new name just in time.

'And your fiancé is the tall Englishman who is so very good at cards? I would call him the handsome Englishman, but I wish us to be friends.'

Petra said this without any hint this was supposed to be a joke. Clemency had met her type before as well, in Bern and in Germany. Her brisk good sense was as typical as her fine cheekbones or her sharp blue eyes. To her, everything would always be clear, without ambiguity. But she would be loyal, and brave, and in her own way, kind.

'This is your first time in Argentina?' she was asking.

Clemency explained their plans, and before long Petra had offered to take her shopping and help her to choose what she would need.

'If you are to be the wife of a rancher, you will need the right clothes. Boots, too. A coat for the days when it rains. We must make a list.'

Soon the party was less intimidating, and Clemency began to enjoy herself. She might not be learning anything useful for Hal, but at least she was helping to build his cover.

She asked Petra about her own life and learned that she had been born in Germany but didn't remember it at all, having come out to Argentina when she was only three.

'Do you ever go back?'

'No,' she said with a hint of regret. 'It takes so long and is so expensive. Also, for my father our country does not have good memories. They were difficult times. When I say that, of course Argentina is now my country.'

Clemency asked whether Petra had anyone in her life who might be on the point of making her an offer of marriage. She said not, said she was content with her life, her friends, her part-time job as a teacher in a kindergarten – and how good she would be at that, Clemency thought. They chatted on until Petra hinted that she might be neglecting her fiancé.

They went into the next room. This had the feel of a casino, with green-baize tables and a sense of pleasurable tension as significant money was wagered on the turn of a card or the fall of a ball. Knots of people gathered to watch, where the sums involved, or the personalities, created the necessary drama. There was a crowd around the table where Hal was sitting. Clemency came to stand behind him and rested her hand on his shoulder in what she hoped was the right mix of familiarity and affection. Absently, he reached up and squeezed her hand, but his eyes never left the man at the far side of the table.

He was in his sixties, strongly-made, with broad shoulders and hair clipped close to his head in a military style. He wore a white linen jacket with a silk cravat, which was surprisingly informal for him and for the place. But it was hard to imagine any of the staff there making any objection, such was his natural authority. He appeared relaxed, but there was a wary look in his eyes as he waited for Hal to place his bet.

Clemency didn't recognise the game they were playing. It had special equipment – a sloping box in which several packs of playing cards were stacked, and a kind of wooden paddle to help move the cards across the wide table. Clemency's mother was a keen bridge player and she could imagine her disdain for this rather theatrical game. Vulgar, she would have said. But it had the excitement of fortunes won and lost. Clemency wondered how much the chips in front of the players were worth.

The cards flowed. A waiter brought drinks for the players. Clemency wished she could see what it was that the others gathered around the table could see – the source of the underlying excitement.

Petra appeared at her side and watched quietly for a couple of hands.

'Your fiancé is a courageous player.' She was speaking softly in her ear so Hal would not hear.

'How can you tell?'

'When he is the bank, he raises the stakes. I think it pleases the General. He finds most of the players here too cautious.'

Now the game came into focus: that the other players were there as a background, part of the audience, while Hal and the man Petra called the General fought their own private duel.

'I did not think the English played *chemin-de-fer*,' the General said to Hal as the bank passed to the right. 'Is it not for you the baccarat, as in America?'

'Oh, some of the private clubs still go in for chemmy,' Hal replied, emphasising the drawl in his voice just a little. 'Of course, the English go to France for the casinos. What about in Germany?'

'I do not know. Everything has changed since the War.'

He said this with the same emphasis with which he turned over his cards. Hal, after lighting a fresh cigarette, picked up the challenge.

'Do you go back much?'

'Never.'

'I don't blame you. You've a damn fine country

here. And Europe's played out.'

The General raised his eyebrows in polite surprise.

'Even your own country?'

'Especially my own country. People like me are prisoners. Exchange controls. If we could take our money out, we'd be off like a shot. A new life in Australia or South Africa.'

'How convenient to have so much of your Empire to settle in. For me, that was not an option.'

Hal tapped the ash from his cigarette before replying.

'The Empire's finished too, you know. We've lost India, and now we're handing Africa over to the blacks. Next it will be the Middle East. Knocks a hole in the thing, don't you think, if there's no longer red white and blue between England and Australia? They'll start to look to America.'

'And England? Will it too look to America, now that Europe is closed to her?'

'God, I hope not. The problem with the Americans is that they only believe in money. Wall Street is their cathedral and the Jewish money-men are their high priests.'

Clemency's face froze. Yet she had to admit he did this very well. It was as if he believed every word.

'Even their religion is big business. For a nation to prosper, I think you have to have faith. Values. Civilisation.'

The card game ran on, but the General's attention was now firmly fixed on this surprising Englishman.

'To what do you ascribe the English malaise?'

'Loss of nerve. That and socialism. Which is only milk and water Communism. The whole country's infected with it. There's even talk of another Labour government, despite what the last one did to us.'

'So you plan to settle on the other side of the world? Is this charming lady to be your wife? I do hope you decide to stay. If I can be of any assistance…'

Clemency had started to wonder if Hal was laying it on too thickly. But it seemed he could have used a trowel, or even a spade, and the General would still have eaten it up. It was, she supposed, exactly what he would have wanted to hear.

But later, she wondered if she were only seeing what she expected. The card game had finished, Hal had settled up and they were having a last drink when Petra found her and drew her to one side to arrange when they should meet to go shopping.

'Your fiancé,' she said cautiously. 'What he said… is it unusual for young men to think this in England?'

'About socialism?' Clemency replied. 'I depends if you're the one who is going to have your land and money taken away, doesn't it? But I don't think too much about it,' she added, remembering her role.

'I know General Haldemann. He is the father of a school friend. I saw you did not like it when they talked about the Jews, and I want you to know that the General is not a…' she searched for the word. 'Not prejudiced. He has many Jewish friends. He agreed with your fiancé from politeness, I think. He would never say such things himself.'

'Are you saying Hal shouldn't either?'

'There would be plenty who would agree with him. But this is a country that no-one can claim as their homeland. Not even the Spanish.'

'That's so nice of you to warn me. Half of what Hal says I just ignore. But I'd hate him to put his foot in it.'

Just then, Hal came over. They collected their coats and walked out to the car. He was in high spirits, and not just because he had taken three hundred pesos off the General, which had led to him promising to stand him lunch one day.

'I picked up a rather interesting piece of information,' Peter added teasingly.

'You certainly laid your cards out,' Clemency said dryly.

'What? Oh, yes, very good. Well, with the German mind I don't think too much subtlety is a good thing.'

'No risk of that.'

'I know what I'm doing,' he said with an edge. 'By the way, do you know who you were chatting to?

'Her name is Petra. She's going to go round the shops with me tomorrow and help me choose what I need for the trip to Misiones. Oh, and she wants you to meet her father.'

'Really? It sounds like you're best friends already. I think you might have an aptitude for this life after all.'

'Why do you say that?'

'That was the lead I picked up tonight. About Werner. After he arrived from Germany, he changed his name to Rausch.'

She stared.

'That's right. Petra Rausch. Reinhard Werner is her father.'

6

Clemency spent the next day with Petra, who was an ideal shopping companion, being very clear in her own mind and full of information about Misiones. Soon Clemency had new clothes, boots, a fetching hat and a sturdy canvas haversack. But any pleasure in spending so much of someone else's money on herself was spoiled by the tension of knowing about Petra's father. Would it be suspicious to ask about him? Or more suspicious not to?

Petra was also so curious about living in swinging London, the latest fashions in music and clothes and books. Fortunately there was not much difference in the lives of Caroline Black and Clemency White, but it was still exhausting, and Clemency was relieved when it was time to part and she could return to the hotel.

Even that was a short-lived respite. It was soon time to change and make her way to the *Bar Clara* for her next lesson. Again, she was put through a gruelling regime for over an hour, until her feet ached and her head span.

She was rewarded with tea, and Lucia, lowering her voice, said that her friend Cristina wished to speak to Clemency discreetly and was expected at any moment. Almost to the minute, there was a knock at the door and Lucia let her in. They kissed like old friends, in what Clemency thought of as the Spanish way, somehow warmer than the French.

'How is your new student?' Cristina asked, and they both turned to look at Clemency.

'She has something,' Lucia conceded. 'Much passion. But it is frozen inside her. I believe she has suffered some great loss.'

This brought Peter so vividly to mind that Clemency found it hard to reply.

'I'm sorry I'm so transparent,' she replied stiffly. 'Maybe I need some acting lessons.'

'But Lucia can help you there too,' Cristina said, highly amused. 'She is an actress as well as a dancer. The toast of the Avenida Corrientes.'

'That is not so,' Lucia protested, a little embarrassed. 'My greatest role was to enter as the maid to tell my master that his wife was returned home and he must hide his mistress under the bed. But this is not why you are here,' she added. 'I will leave you alone.'

'I have no secrets from Lucia,' Cristina explained, as the door closed. 'I would trust her with my life. But she prefers to know nothing, and it is better so.'

'I suppose it is.'

'I wished to see you today because I have a message for your colleague who is so busy. Do you know of the work of the Link?'

'No.'

Just as at their last meeting, Cristina was annoyed at Clemency's ignorance about her country, but also moved swiftly to remedy it.

'When the Nazis came here, they created the Link to look after each other. My country has many such societies. You pay in a few pesos a week, and if you fall ill, then they will pay for a doctor, or if you die, they will look after your children. But this went much further. They wished to protect themselves at every level – police, judges, all the way to the *Casa Rosada*. The President's Palace,' she added impatiently.

'Perón.'

'Very good. And within the Link, there was another group. The *Wachhund*. A society within a society. It looked for those who were enemies of the Nazis. It worked against them. Spying and subversion. Intimidation. Sometimes, even murder. All to protect the Link.'

'And it's still going?'

'Oh yes. Not so much as before. But after Eichmann, it has become strong again. No-one likes to think they will walk down the street one day and be in Tel Aviv the next, answering for their crimes. There are men who will pay a great deal for their security. There is money to bribe. Also, some of those in the Link are also in the police or in S.I.D.E., or in the Federal Ministry of Justice. They can call on these men at any time for help.'

'Would the *Wachhund* know about Mr Linklater?'

'Perhaps. It is hard to say. If he is working with S.I.D.E. or the police, then yes, they probably know he is a British agent. If not, and he is clever, then he may not be exposed.'

'What about you?'

'Me? Oh, they know me. For now, they think it is making more trouble to kill me than to not.'

She said this calmly, but how easy would that be to live with? Clemency had herself experienced the fear of exposure, arrest, torture. But that had only been for a few days at a time, and she had her own country to return to. How much worse to be at risk your whole life, never knowing if one day the calculation might change, and you would end up on a death list.

'I have two things I would like you to take to Señor Linklater,' Lucia was saying. 'The first is this message, that he should be very careful who he speaks to in S.I.D.E. If he wishes, he could tell me who he is thinking of contacting, and I can ask those I know and say if it is safe or not. You understand?'

'Of course. And the other?'

'The Link is not the only secret group in my country. There are many working to expose the Nazis. With you British, with your money and your influence, perhaps we could do more. Maybe one day you will tell me what you are doing here, you and your Sir Linklater. Maybe one day I will find out for myself. But to help you decide to work with us, I have a gift. If you have come to find Nazis, there is one I think you will want to take home with you.'

She drew out a slim folder and handed it over.

'May I read it?' Clemency asked.

'You think I believe that you are just the new girl at the Embassy?' Cristina replied with a smile. 'Of course, if you work with Señor Linklater then you may read it. But not now. I will tell you the story. It does not take long.'

She leant even closer.

'In the second war, there were many of your pilots who were in a camp. They planned an escape, a hundred of them or more, I think. And they were caught, almost all of them, as they knew they would be. But then the Nazis changed the rules. They did not say, bad luck old boy, well played, you must go back into the camp again.'

Clemency smiled at Cristina's approximation of a British accent; and then she realised what was coming next.

'You remember? They took fifty of these men. Prisoners of war. They took them to a field and they shot them all dead. Murdered them.'

She tapped the folder.

'This is the man who was in charge.'

◊

That evening, as she ate her meal in her room, bathed and dressed and packed her bag for the night in the archive, her mind kept returning to the file lying at the bottom of her suitcase. She was sure Hal would be impressed; but it was hot in her hands, too important, too dangerous.

As they drove through the city, she repeated what Cristina had told her about the Link, and the infiltration of S.I.D.E.

'Don't worry about that,' he said dismissively. 'I've no intention of going within a hundred miles of them. In this kind of caper, safety is in the fewer people who know you're there. In fact, I'm wondering if it was a mistake for you and me to be involved with Navarra. Of course, we just don't have the manpower out here. But even so… She could turn into a liability. I always worry about people who believe in things.'

'You believe in things,' she protested.

'Queen and country? That's different. Anyway, let's hope she doesn't blow up in our faces.'

'You might change your mind when you see this.'

She produced the file. With a hint of a sigh, he found somewhere to stop. Then he flicked through it, then read it again, much more carefully. His face gave nothing away.

'Well?'

'It's good stuff. I'll need to talk to Catsmeat. But it'll need to wait.'

'Why?'

'Because this is your last night in the salt mines. Tomorrow we pack our tents and slip away.'

'Really? Where are we going?'

He started the car again and slipped back into the traffic.

'Misiones.'

◊

Clemency was relieved to have a final night in the archives. Cristina's words had set off a train of thought that might lead her to identify some of the Nazi sympathisers within the Argentinian government. Each application for an entry visa needed sponsors, and if the same names kept coming up, then they must be part of an organised network.

And so it proved. Soon she was covering pages of her notebook with names, dates, addresses, not only of the sponsors, but the other applications they had supported. Dozens of names, and still they came, so that she was rushing to get them all down, conscious of time passing. She felt like a thief presented with a dragon's hoard, too much wealth to carry away, hardly able to choose what to take.

The last hour before she was due to meet Hal passed in a blur, but finally she had packed her notes away, climbed back up to the window and was back out on the roof, breathing in the fresh, sea-scented air. It was quiet, still, but even the distant city sounds were loud after the tomb-like silence of the archive.

She let herself down by the rope, then unhitched it and

slid it free, so she would leave no trace of her presence. She was winding it up when she heard a footfall behind her. She turned with a flippant comment to Hal about his leaving her to do all the work, when she saw two men approaching her down the alley, a little apart, so that there was no way past them.

She backed away, taking in something about the way they walked, a little crouched over, hands held out, that frightened her.

Then she saw the glint of metal. A knife.

They weren't police, or security. They couldn't be ordinary criminals, either. Who would come looking for a victim in this isolated spot, in the dead hour before dawn?

She stepped further back. Then there were arms around her, pinning her. She tried to break free, but the man behind her was too strong, and before she could cry out the others were on her and one had a gloved hand pressed over her mouth.

A knife at her throat. She stopped struggling.

They began to march her towards the road. But then they stopped, sizing up the man who stood in their way.

Hal.

Two of them approached him. He slipped off his jacket and held it loose in one hand.

The first of the men dropped into a half-crouch, and began to come closer.

She couldn't understand why Hal didn't have his gun. One sight of that and the men would scatter. How could he think to take on three of them, unarmed?

The first man lunged forward. Hal spun his jacket round and the man slid by him, his arm tangled. And Hal had him round the neck and in a moment there was a crack and the man began to scream. Hal let him drop to his knees, where he crouched over, holding his broken arm and cursing.

She stared in shock. It had been so quick and so simple, like wringing a bird's neck.

The two other men were stunned too, and Clemency took her chance, jabbing the one holding her in the face with her elbow, then slipping free. She ran and took the knife that the injured man had dropped, and Hal flashed her a smile.

The man who had held her was approaching. His injured companion was swearing at him, and telling him to come away. Clemency took a pace towards him, remembering now what she had been taught in far-off Bern, about taking on a man with a knife. Confidence was everything. That, and footwork. She danced to his left, a little nearer, but leaving him a way of escape.

And he took it. Soon there were just three men running away, one still moaning in pain.

Hal came over to her, brushing his jacket. He took the flick-knife from her, folded it up and slipped it into his pocket.

'Friends of yours?'

'Thank you,' she said carefully, feeling shaky, her fear catching up with her.

'All part of the service,' he replied. 'One thing, though. When we get back to the hotel, would you mind sewing this up for me?'

He showed her the jacket, where the man's knife had sliced through the silk lining.

'Bit awkward to explain to the concierge, eh?'

7

Hal had hired a Cadillac 62, by far the most luxurious car Clemency had ever ridden in, with air conditioning and power steering and deep cushioned seats with proper headrests. Once they'd shaken off the suburbs of Buenos Aires, it sat at sixty for mile after mile along Highway 4. Soon Clemency dozed off. The busy days preparing for the trip, accompanying Hal to social events and her tango lessons, had tired her out. The shock of the night's events had left her exhausted.

She only woke when it was time for lunch, and already the landscape had changed. It was hotter, humid, the vegetation lush and the soil the colour of terracotta. They stopped at a restaurant on the edge of the Uruguay River, a vast spread of cocoa-brown water oozing slowly by. But despite this, the fish was beautifully fresh. Hal was soon on his second glass of wine, and decided it was time to give Clemency a lecture on Nazi-hunting.

'I don't know if you have a picture in your mind. Perhaps someone like the General back at the *Bavaria*. But Ullmann is nothing like that. The last description we have of him, from about ten years ago, says that he's thin, balding, short-sighted and has a bit of a stoop. Not exactly the Master Race. Anyway, he taught History of Art and when the war came and he was going to be called up he sorted out a quiet berth for himself on the staff of Hermann Goring, who as I am sure you know was head of the Luftwaffe.'

Clemency hadn't known that. Anything about the Nazis, she had always found deadly dull, like the endless war films they churned out at Shepperton and Ealing.

'So our friend Ullmann is drawn into helping Fat Hermann put together one of the largest and finest collections of art the world has ever seen, almost all of it looted through conquest or stolen from Jews. I think along the way he managed to do some dealing on his own account and also knew how to get the money out of Germany and into a currency that would survive the war. When the end came, he presumably bribed someone to get the right papers and tipped up here in Argentina.'

'Why is he so important?'

'I can't tell you that. I probably shouldn't be telling you any of this. But it might be helpful. You see, it's likely he still has some connection to the world of art, isn't it? Perhaps he's dealing in antiques or local artefacts, or maybe he works for a museum or an auction house. He's likely to have changed his name again, so this might be the only way to track him down.'

'Even that sounds like a long shot.'

The long morning's drive, which had taken them not even half-way to the border of the province of Misiones, made her realise just how difficult their task was.

'We're not entirely alone. On this trip, it's you, me and the Bank of England.' He smiled at her puzzlement. 'The Treasury have authorised some pretty hefty expenditure, if I need it. If anyone knows the real identities of their better-off residents, it will be the local chiefs of police. Some pesos in the right place and they'll be happy to let me know where Ullmann is hiding. After that, it will be down to me. To us.'

'What will you do to him?'

'I don't know,' Hal said. 'I don't want any fuss. That might scare off Werner or Zoll. Let's just say that whatever happens to Ullmann, it will be no more than he deserves.'

'What then?'

'We go after the other two. At least with Werner, we know where he is. Zoll is more of a worry. We may need to put you back into the archive for you to do some more digging.'

'Isn't that a bit risky?'

'Scared? That's not like you.'

'I'm only thinking of the mission,' she said, but that wasn't wholly true. Hal had reassured her that the men who had tried to seize her must have been members of the *Wachhund* tipped off about an intruder poking around the archive, without having any idea who she was. Otherwise, they wouldn't have been taken by surprise by Hal's appearance. It made sense, but she still felt anxious. And surely they would be expecting her to return?

'It's all about risks and rewards,' he was saying. 'If we can't get after Zoll any other way, we'll just have to push things a bit. But as I said, one thing at a time.'

'So we'll deal with Werner when we're back in Buenos Aires?'

He drained his glass.

'All in good time, darling. Let's get going.'

The set off and the miles ran on, only the rumble of

the car's massive engine for company. They stopped for petrol at a ramshackle garage, miles from the nearest town. The attendant was young, good-looking, as aloof and glamorous as a racing driver. He was too proud to do more than nod at them. But he spent as long as he could on filling the tank, checking the oil, polishing the windscreen with a rag, all to earn a tip or perhaps just to spread out this rare moment of human contact.

Another hour on the road and she could see Hal's eyes beginning to glaze over. She knew he would snap at her if she said he should rest, or that she could drive, so instead she searched round for more conversation.

'I'll tell you a funny thing about Pryce-Jones. I think he's planning to have an affair.'

'Planning?' Hal thought about this. 'Yes, I suppose he would plan it. Nothing spur of the moment about Catsmeat. Who's the lucky girl? Not you, I hope?'

'Lord, no. You know the tango lessons I'm having? He was asking about my teacher in a way that was just a bit too casual. As if he wanted to know everything about her, but without my noticing.'

'And what is she like?'

'She's about my height, with bobbed black hair and—'

'I mean her character. Would you trust her?'

Clemency's mind filled with paradoxes: passionate and worldly-wise, selfish and generous, impulsive and calculating. It made the real Lucia hard to describe.

'She's very Argentinian,' she said lamely. But this seemed enough.

'Ah! Beautiful and dangerous. Caressing you one moment and sticking a knife in you the next. If you were married to Venetia Pryce-Jones, you might want some of that. That must be like going to bed with a marble statue.'

Clemency couldn't think of anything to say in reply to that, but Hal was now happily chatting away.

'You'll have to introduce us when we're back in BA. She sounds like hot stuff, and certainly needs to be saved from Catsmeat's clutches.'

'I couldn't do that. You see, I like her.'

'Ho, ho. Well, don't worry, I can do my own seducing. Where does she live?'

'Above a café called *Bar Clara*.'

'Is there a man in the background? I don't want some pimp breaking in on us with a flick-knife.'

'She's not like that,' Clemency protested, but Hal kept on, asking about Lucia's friends, how she spent her time, apparently finding it highly amusing to learn all he could about his future mistress. It was the same kind of over-curiosity that Pryce-Jones had shown, though in his case he'd pretended to be encouraging Clemency to experience the native culture. Was every Argentinian she met to be an object of suspicion? Lucia could hardly be an agent of the Link, because it was Cristina who had introduced her. And yet…

The logic appeared sound; but it did not reassure her.

◊

They drove in silence for an hour, and then another, until suddenly Hal was pulling over to the side of the road by a shack selling fruit, the big car wallowing over the rough ground to a halt. With the engine stopped, it was suddenly very quiet.

He returned with a string bag full of oranges,

presumably grown in the orchards that lined the road. They set off straight away and she began to peel them and feed him segments, until her handkerchief was sodden with juice.

'You know how much that bag was?' he asked. 'The equivalent of tuppence. This is a country where, with some foreign currency, you can live like a king. Everything's like that. Land. Beef. Wine. You can see why they came here.'

She thought of Petra, and her hollow assurance that she was an Argentine now, even when the Germany she could not remember filled her mind. Like a fish, once you had the hook in your mouth, you couldn't quite break free. However far you swam, however much line was paid out, in the end, exhausted, it would draw you back.

She tried to express some of this to Hal, but he waved it aside.

'Plenty of others would swop places with them,' he pronounced. 'Including the millions who died in the war. They might feel sorry for themselves now, the Germans, but at the end of the day, they started it, didn't they?'

She had no desire to argue with him, and would have let it drop, but her efforts to change the subject only annoyed him. He wanted the argument, wanted to win it. He pulled out his wallet and took out a photograph. It was a studio portrait of a man in his late fifties, serious behind his thick rimmed glasses, thoughtful, perhaps a hint of kindness behind the professional image. A family lawyer, perhaps, or a doctor.

'That's Reinhard Werner, he said. 'A model citizen, wouldn't you say?'

She looked again at the image. She could see

nothing of Petra in it. Except perhaps the firmness and
certainty about the eyes.

'He's one of the top Nazi war criminals, you know.'

'Yes, but what did he actually do?' She was curious
to know, and also desperate not to hear.

'He's an engineer by training. Specialised in
industrial processes. Designing factories, chemical
plants, that kind of thing. When the war came, he
joined the Luftwaffe and was put on to building
airfields. He could design them so that everything
worked more efficiently – maintenance, refuelling,
and so on. Like a production line. Then he turns up
on air defences in '42, overseeing the installation of
dozens of Wurzburg radar sites. He must have caught
the eye of someone senior, because he's switched to
RHSA IV to work on a particularly important project
in Poland.'

He said this as if this told the whole story. She
had no idea what RHSA was or why it mattered, but
admitting her ignorance always put Hal in a good
mood. He set off on a long explanation that ranged
over the whole inner workings of the SS and the
Gestapo, the Wannersee Conference and the General
Government, and which ended with her learning that
Werner was one of the engineers who designed the
death camps used for murdering millions of people.

'Imagine living with that on your conscience,'
Clemency said.

'He seems to be coping,' Hal replied dryly. 'After
all, if you were prepared to be part of that in the first
place, you can probably deal with the knowledge
afterwards.'

Perhaps it was the long drive, or the heat, but
Clemency had trouble sleeping that night. She

lay awake, listening to the faint breeze in the trees outside, and thought about Petra, and whether she ever suspected that she had been fathered by a monster.

8

San Fernando was cluttered and scruffy, with every wall shedding plaster to reveal the breeze-blocks beneath, sagging iron roofs, the roads broken up and pot-holed, a raw new home thrown up next to a half-ruin. But it was also lush and green, trees and shrubs in every garden, creepers pouring over the walls and cascading into the streets, feeling their way over the rooftops and along telephone wires and round the ironwork of gates and balconies. There could be no greater contrast with the order and neatness of Bern, or of her own home village, and yet Clemency loved it.

They drove slowly down the main street. A dog lay in the dust, sunning itself, while a couple of men, stocky and with heavy moustaches, in colourful short-sleeved shirts and wide-brimmed hats, broke off their conversation to watch them pass. There was one hotel, dozing in the afternoon heat much like the dog, but looking clean and inviting, the interior shadowy and cool. The manager himself appeared at the reception desk and dealt briskly with the paperwork, then showed them to their rooms on the first floor, clearly the best the *Hotel Paraná* could offer. Clemency's room was filled with dark mahogany furniture, the intricate carvings ingrained with dust, but the bed was aired, and there was water in the taps.

They dined in the hotel's courtyard, making an

effort to chat about anything except their mission and finding how little they had in common when it came to books, or films, or politics. There were rumours of an election coming up in the spring, and Hal spent most of the evening explaining why electing Harold Wilson would be a disaster for the country, and assuming that Clemency would agree with him.

She held her tongue, except to wonder aloud if the current lot were any better. But even suggesting that Labour would make a change from all the sex scandals, and the spying scandals, and indeed the sex-and-spying scandals, Hal saw as heresy. She had to suffer more dull minutes as he put her right. She wondered if this was the effect of his being outside the UK so much – an occupational hazard with being an officer in SIS – this lack of perspective, this seeing everything in such stark terms, in which the unions were riddled with Communists and Labour were tools of the Kremlin.

'All these clever grammar school boys at the BBC, mocking everything from the monarchy down. They won't look so clever when the Red Army marches in, will they?'

There was more, much more, of this, and it was a relief when dinner was over. The only positive was that he had been too busy explaining how the world worked to make another pass at her.

The next day, Hal thought it would look odd if she accompanied him on his visits to the local bigwigs – the Mayor, the Chief of Police and so on. Instead, she spent the morning in her room, where from the writing desk she could look down the length of the main street and watch the life of the place ebb and flow. She'd had so little spare time since arriving in Argentina, and she was soon thinking of Peter. Swan

had told her he would be treated well enough. After
all, he was an asset the Soviets would want to swap
for one of their own agents, now in the hands of the
British. But she hated the thought of him in prison,
isolated, subject to interrogation. They might not
torture him, but they would do everything else they
could to break his spirit.

And all the time, she was out here, enjoying herself.
Yes, she was here because of Peter. And yes, there
was danger. But a voice at the back of her mind was
telling her she should be sitting at home, crying into
a handkerchief and counting the days until her man
returned, not jetting half-way around the world to
pretend to take his place.

Hal returned with some introductions to local
landowners, and after lunch they set off. The sun
was strong and she was glad of her cool cotton dress
and her wide-brimmed straw hat, though once they
reached the edge of the town and Hal put his foot
on the gas, she had to keep a hand clamped on it to
stop it blowing away. He was bare-headed, but had
produced a pair of aviator sunglasses that made him
look alarmingly like an officer in the CIA.

They had a map, but it was sketchy, showing only
the larger rivers and the main roads, so that it was
hard to know whether the many tracks that led off
into the flat farmland led to the next village, or one of
the many *estancia*, or would peter out into nothing.
They tried asking the way from the workers in the
fields, but were usually met by incomprehension, real
or feigned, as if they were aliens who had come from
outer space in a vast American car. When they did find
the estates they were searching for, they were always
welcomed warmly, but enjoying their hospitality took

time. By the end of the day, they were hot and tired, over-full of tea and pastries and no nearer their quarry.

Mostly they drove in silence. It wasn't hostile or unfriendly: there just wasn't much to say which they hadn't already exchanged in the days before. Once or twice Hal asked about her background, her family, and her work in Bern, and they would chat for a while. But she got little in return when she asked about his life – a few airy comments about it all being too dull for words. It needled her a little, as if he wanted to remind her that he was the boss.

'I've been thinking...' she began.

'Sounds ominous.'

'About Zoll. Wouldn't he want to try and reconstruct his old life, as much as he could? Like Werner. He was an engineer, designing factories, and in Argentina he's built several abattoirs, which are just another kind of factory. Wouldn't Zoll either be practising as a doctor or teaching medicine?'

'So? Every small town has a doctor. He could still be anywhere.'

'Yes, but if he's a doctor – a medical doctor – he'd need to be on a register, wouldn't he? They're bound to have the equivalent of the General Medical Council or the BMA. It would take a while to go through them all and trace them, but it might be a start. Or maybe he'd just like the atmosphere in a university town. So maybe he's in Cordoba.'

'Why there?'

'It's the second-oldest university in the Americas. Only Harvard goes back further.'

'You do know some odd things,' Hal said indulgently.

'What if we found out who his colleagues were back in Germany, and whether any of them are now working at a university in Argentina? He's hardly likely to be in the same place, so we could eliminate a lot of options and narrow it down.'

'Sounds like a lot of work. How would we get those kinds of records?'

'London could do it.'

He didn't bother replying. His whole attitude was detached, almost amused, as if he knew exactly where Zoll was but enjoyed hearing her try and work it out. She'd had teachers like that – whose pleasure was to know more than their pupils, not to educate them – and she hadn't liked any of them.

◊

She woke suddenly, alert and a little afraid. Apart from the sound of the crickets, the hotel was silent. She couldn't sense anyone in the room. Then came the muffled sound of voices, and the creak of a floorboard.

Her room was dark, the windows shuttered. She guessed it was about two in the morning. Another creak, two or three in a row, perhaps footsteps, perhaps not. She thought of how obvious they had been, breezing into Misiones and trying to insert themselves into the German community. The *Wachhund* had been set up in part to deal with exactly this kind of threat. And the *Wachhund*, she suspected, would be very efficient.

There was a heavy thud on the other side of the wall, behind her head. Hal's room. She eased back the single sheet, ready to go to his aid, wishing she'd insisted on having a gun.

Then the sounds returned, a rhythmic creaking, a grunt, a woman's voice, and Clemency blushed. Not a fight, not a struggle. He was in bed with a woman.

It went on for several minutes, surprisingly clear, from the creak of the springs to the rap of the headboard against the wall, his muffled words, her cries of ecstasy. Clemency felt ashamed to be listening, like the aural equivalent of a Peeping Tom, and yet also furious that she should have to hear it. And she hated the animal sounds, the thought that if she and Peter had gone to bed in the hotel in Paris – and how she'd wanted them to – the guests in the next room would have been treated to the same performance.

At last it was over, and then there was silence, and then a low rumble of voices for a surprisingly long time, and then she fell asleep again.

In the morning, she was down to breakfast first and as soon as she took her seat, was convinced that everyone else in the hotel, from the elderly couple at the next table to the waitress bringing her coffee, were laughing up their sleeves at her. Did they think that was her voice in the night, crying out in passion? Or did they know that it was her fiancé, the man whom she expected to take a vow to love and honour her, who was screwing a girl in the room next to hers, and making sure she heard how much they were enjoying themselves?

She drank her coffee, but the food stuck in her throat.

At last Hal appeared, looking relaxed, and pleased with himself.

'Hello darling,' he said. 'Sleep all right?'

'Yes, darling,' she replied. 'And you?'

'Like a log.'

◊

The next few days followed the same pattern. Hal would have a list of properties to visit, and they would set off into the countryside, alternating between the harsh sunshine on the road and the cool shade of a veranda, chatting to the owners or the managers about land that might be for sale. Back in the hotel, they would dine early, and part for the night, and Clemency would have the queasy knowledge that at some point she would be woken by Hal's lovemaking through the thin wall between their bedrooms.

There was no shortage of leads for them to pursue, though Hal didn't explain where they came from. There were also more chances to meet local landowners socially because the Mayor had decided to be helpful – or perhaps, given he was also the local lawyer, did not want to see a potential client settle elsewhere – and arranged more introductions. One day, a land agent took them on a trek into the *campo*, so they could get a feel for the country. The next, the son of the town clerk took them sailing on the Paraná. On the Saturday, there was an *asada* at a nearby ranch, where most of the local society – other ranchers, land agents, merchants, doctors and lawyers – had gathered, many of them German immigrants. This led to more introductions, more invites, and for the first time Hal's plan of posing as an English landowner began to bear fruit. If Ullmann's family were still living in the district, they were bound to meet them, or at least hear about them.

Unless Ullman heard about them first.

9

As a child, Clemency had learned to ride. In her part of the world, it's what people like her did. But she had never been horsey. She hadn't read pony stories under the bedclothes or spent every hour she could mucking out stables for a pittance, just to be near the beasts. Sometimes it was fun to go for a hack through the woods, and she been hunting a few times and liked the admiring glances she won in her midnight-blue coat, but rubbing the horse down afterwards was a tedious chore. Fundamentally, a horse wasn't as good as a car. You couldn't go to the shops, or a party, or run up to town. So, for years the place in her heart that might have been given over to Lucky or Thunder had been filled by dreams of Alfas and Jaguars and was now more realistically occupied by the Austin Mini.

But as she jogged comfortably along one of the farm tracks that cross-crossed the *campo*, under a warm sun, with a pleasant breeze, her mare at least as happy with life as she was, she had to admit it was better than driving. It was a warm day, blue skies, and at last she had the chance to wear the black jodhpurs and loose white shirt and the broad-brimmed black riding hat that Petra had helped her to pick in far-off Buenos Aires.

With a horse, you had a better view, for one thing; but even more, you could feel and smell. The heat

rising from the rich earth. The sharp sweet scent from
the citrus trees. Even the farm workers seemed more
human, less remote, as they worked their way through
the fields, the thick yellow heads of the maize falling
to the swathe of their machetes.

The object of her ride was the *Casa Anna*, the home
of a Señor Karslichter, who was apparently known
as one of the foremost collectors of native art in the
region, but it was as much a chance to spend some
time on her own. Hal had arranged a weekly trip to
Campo Grande to report securely to Pryce-Jones.
When he offered her the choice whether to make the
six-hour journey or not, she chose not. She wondered
if he realised that, each night, she was disturbed by
the sounds of his sexual prowess.

At least his own mood had improved. Perhaps the
sex was a release for him from the stresses of the
mission. Back in BA, the idea of the hunted becoming
the hunters had seemed far-fetched. Here in Misiones,
with the German community so strong and so settled
into the fabric of the country, dining with the Mayor
and drinking with the Chief of Police, they were
horribly exposed.

She had reached the crest of a low hill and now
could see beyond a line of poplars the red-tiled roofs
and high whitewashed walls of an *estancia*. In the
heat of the day, the prospect of tea or lemonade in the
shade was very welcome, more so than the remote
chance that yet another German settler might turn out
to to be Ullmann. But as she and her horse ambled up
to the entrance to the compound, and she noticed just
how tall and well-maintained were the walls she was
passing through, Clemency became a little pensive.
Hal was over a hundred miles away.

She stopped a little way from the steps leading to the veranda and took her time dismounting and tying up her horse. After a few moments a man in a white linen suit waved to her in greeting, and then came over, carefully setting his Panama hat on his head. It gave him a neat appearance a little at odds with the usual style of the farm-owners.

'My name is Braun,' he said as he boed to her. 'I very much regret that Herr Karslichter is away. I expect him back this evening.'

She explained that she had met Herr Karslichter briefly at a party and, as she happened to be passing, had stopped by to renew the acquaintance. Braun insisted on providing the hospitality his friend would no doubt have offered.

They walked together towards the house. Braun was older than she'd first thought, at least sixty, though still fit, with tanned skin and sharp blue eyes. Clemency was sure that his jet-black hair wasn't natural, but she could forgive a certain amount of vanity because his conversation was entertaining and he had some old-world courtesy, leading her to a patch of shade.

'I have heard from my friend Karslichter about the two young English who think of settling in this district. But your fiancé? He could not be with you today?'

'He had some business in Campo Grande,' she replied. 'He'll be back later on.'

'A man has a fiancée who is as charming as you, yet he leaves you behind?' Braun had adopted the clumsy joviality that many men of his age seemed to think appropriate with her generation. 'I must admit I do not understand the young people of today.'

He shook his head in mock disbelief, but Clemency

noted the sharpness of his gaze and thought again
about how visible the trail that she and Hal had laid
must be, for this man to know so much about them.

He was a pleasant and cultured companion, talking
knowledgably about the Guarani and early Jesuit
works that were Karslichter's main stock in trade, and
which formed the thin excuse for Clemency's visit. It
turned out that Braun too was a dealer in antiquities.
As it took him over a wide swathe of Argentina, Brazil
and Paraguay, he offered himself as another source of
information on where they should look for their new
home.

When Clemency showed more than polite interest
in fine art, he insisted on showing her over the house.
The rooms were well-proportioned, cool and light,
protected from the sun by the veranda that ran around
all four sides but with plenty of large windows and
wide, high doorways giving in to the central rooms.
Every available space was filled with paintings,
engravings, statues or cabinets displaying fine
porcelain. It was hard to image how all these treasures
– and they included many that were European –
had found their way to this remote corner of South
America.

Braun was obviously on the closest terms with
Karslicher, because the tour included his study. This
too was shaded from the sun by the veranda, but it was
no cool and refreshing sanctuary from the heat outside.
The dark wooden floor, the heavy oak furniture,
the rows of leather-bound books, even the sombre
paintings, made it gloomy and oppressive. It also had
the feeling of a museum; as if no fire were ever lit
in the grate, and the long velvet curtains were never
drawn. It was a room to withdraw into and brood.

'I must show you this,' Braun said, leading them to a landscape in an ornate gilt frame hanging on the far wall. 'It is by Wissel.'

The picture was too sentimental for her taste. It showed a mountain crag, with wind-wracked pines clinging to its sides, and beyond, lit by fitful sunlight, distant fields of rich fruitfulness.

'It's very dramatic,' she said. 'Where is it of?'

'Pomerania,' Braun replied, pleased by her apparent enthusiasm. 'Here is a portrait by Werner Peiner. An early work of his, but still good, I think. And over here…'

Clemency sensed that he was puzzled by her, wanted to know more, was reluctant for her to go before he had his answer. The insistence on showing off these treasures might be an act, a chance to continue their conversation, to observe her, to probe gently about her background, and what she and Hal were doing in San Fernando.

They returned to the veranda, and the servants had laid out iced juice and pastries. They talked of art, music, the primaries of the US elections, Goldwater and Rockefeller, and Clemency sat back, not needing to say much when Braun had such certain views. All she could think of was how isolated she was, here in the deep countryside. They were alone there, except for the farm workers, and out here, in this semi-feudal world, Karslichter was their lord and master, not the local mayor or police chief, let alone the distant government in Brasilia. If she were to disappear, they would ask no questions themselves, and answer none put by anyone else.

Finally, they were done, and Braun was helping her back into the saddle. He still seemed unwilling to let her go, and she had to promise to return, bringing Hal with her.

She took the track back towards San Fernando, suddenly exhausted. It was partly the heat of the day and the prospect of the long ride back, but there was also the release of tension, now that she was outside the walls of the *Casa Anna*.

The shadows were lengthening, but it was still hot and she did not feel that she, or the horse, could make much speed. It was frustrating, though. She wanted desperately to see Hal. Partly, she had to admit, it would be reassuring to be under his wing once more. But there was another reason.

She had found Ullmann.

◊

At first, Hal was far from convinced, but he was in a good mood despite his long drive and didn't dismissed Clemency's suspicions.

'I was lucky I met Braun,' she said. 'Karslichter wouldn't have shown me his study, I'm sure of that. It was so revealing. The rest of the house was how he wanted to be seen by others, but the study was the real him. An exile mourning the country where he could never return.'

'We've met plenty of those.'

'Yes, but it was the pictures. He had a portrait by Zeigler. He was Hitler's favourite painter. Did you know that?'

'So he's a Nazi. That doesn't get us much further forward.'

'It's more than that. At the very least, it all still matters to him. He's not someone who was caught up in it all back in the war and has made a new life in Argentina. He's still in the club. And maybe more. Maybe it's like showing a badge or having a secret handshake. The paintings are a way to prove which side you're on.'

'Don't run ahead of yourself,' Hal said, amused by her enthusiasm but also accepting there might just be something in it.

'Would you put a bet on it?'

'I thought you didn't bet.'

'A shilling says he's Ullmann.'

'What do you know?' he asked suspiciously. 'Oh, go on, then. A shilling. Now, spit it out.'

'There was another painting. A mountain-top. A place called the Löwenberg. That's near Königsberg, which is where Ullmann was born. The painting would be a connection back to those days – but a fairly safe one.'

'Not safe enough. But maybe he couldn't have foreseen the cleverest girl in the world coming to visit.'

Clemency just smiled.

'So we go back?' he said, half to himself. 'Make an offer on the *Estancia las Palmas*? That would give us an excuse for calling on him again, if we're about to become neighbours. Maybe asking around in the neighbourhood a bit more.'

'Won't it be the same problem? He's more likely to learn about us than we are to learn about him.'

'Yes. Perhaps we know all we need to know. Did you notice the walls, by the way?'

For the next half-hour, he questioned her on every detail of the *Casa Anna*. There were things she hadn't thought much of at the time, because many of the

other *estancias* had them: but put together, it was
both formidable and suspicious. Broken glass along
the tops and some powerful floodlights. A pair of
Doberman Pinschers restless in a cage. A gun room
with enough rifles for an army.

'How are we going to get at him?' she asked, half-
afraid he would remember her experience in burglary,
and push her over the wall alone.

'Yes, it's a bit of a poser, isn't it? What would you
do?'

This caught her off-guard. She suggested trying to
kidnap him when he drove into San Fernando, or even
shooting him with a hunting rifle from some distant
vantage-point. It all seemed rather improbable, as
well as extremely dangerous. Even if they got him,
how would they get away afterwards.

'I hadn't realised quite how bloodthirsty you are,'
Hal said. 'Are you casting me in the role of assassin,
or is this another of your many skills?'

'Well, I'd go to the local police. But you tell me we
can't.'

'I didn't say that exactly. But the main thing is for
us to start to fade out of San Fernando. We'll let it be
known we're going to start looking on the Paraguayan
side of the Paraná. And that we're going to Asunción
for a couple of days to see what we can find out there
about places that may be coming onto the market.
OK?'

◊

Hal was absent for the whole of the next day, and
Clemency had nothing to do but sit in her room and
catch up on some letter-writing. They had arranged to

dine together as usual, but when she had bathed and changed and was about to knock on Hal's door, a man in uniform emerged. He was in his thirties, with dark eyes and a closely-trimmed moustache, immaculately turned out from his brightly-polished cap badge to his gleaming boots. He smiled at her as he passed, wished her a good evening, but there was some extra meaning in his glance.

She found Hal tidying away a couple of glasses and a bottle of whisky, still nearly full.

'Who was that?' she asked.

'That was Captain Lopez, of the Federal Police.'

'He seemed very pleased with life.'

'We had a very profitable exchange. I know a little more about one of the local residents, for one thing.'

He gave no more explanation but took down his suitcase.

'Where are we going?' she asked.

'Paraguay. Oh, and this is yours.'

He fished something from his pocket and threw it to her. Something small and shiny. She caught it instinctively, one-handed, then opened her palm. A coin. A shilling.

10

They set off after breakfast towards distant Asunción before finding a side road that would take them in a wide loop back to the Paraná about twenty miles south of San Fernando. The traffic was light, and on the long straight road they could easily overtake the labouring trucks and buses, and skim past the more frequent donkey carts that placidly hugged the side of the road.

Hal kept an eye out for anything that might be following them, including making a couple of stops in wayside cafés to see who came past and whether their tail – if there were one – could resist the temptation to study them as they passed.

'The problem is, there's really only one way to Asunción.' He moved their glasses of sickly lemonade and flattened out the map. 'If they really wanted to keep tabs on us, they'd pick us up on the way, here or maybe here.'

They were sitting in the shade, but the heat was still fierce, all the more so now there was no breeze from driving. Clemency wished she'd ordered bottled water. The lemonade – so sweet, and such a strange colour – was furring her teeth.

'What do we do when we get to the ferry?' She'd resisted asking him during the drive, knowing he never wanted to confide in her. But the operation was only hours away.

'How are you with guns?'

He'd asked something similar when they first met, but that had been casual, showing off on his part. This was clearly for real.

'You won't need to shoot anyone,' he went on. 'Just make some noise.'

'I could do that,' she replied. 'What sort of gun?'

'I'll show you later. Look, you see the river here, where it comes round in this curve. And the road over here? That's where the ferry is. It's not much more than an overgrown punt with an old man who will take you across the river for fifty centavos. You could just about fit a bicycle on it, but no more than that. Of course, there's no guards or paperwork. You're in Paraguay, no questions asked.

'I'm sure that one of the reasons that Ullmann is based here is that he's got the river, and safety, behind him. It's less than ten miles from his *estancia* to the crossing. He's got to go out that way.'

'Yes, but why tonight? Is he meeting someone?'

'Better than that.' Hal produced his wolfish smile. 'Captain Lopez and I have come to an arrangement. He's now convinced that Ullmann is involved in the smuggling trade. As a captain of police, it is his duty to investigate, whatever powerful friends Ullmann might have. At dawn tomorrow, he's going to raid the *Casa Anna*. He'll have a dozen Federal police and there'll be roadblocks up all round. If he can manage it, there'll also be a light plane on standby in case Ullmann makes off across country.'

'But he's going to warn Ullmann just in time, and Ullmann will head straight to the ferry.'

She'd meant to sound enthusiastic. But the way she'd guessed the next stage so easily annoyed him.

'There's a bit more to it than that,' he said, an edge in his voice. 'If he's arrested at the ferry, it will look like we were acting in concert with Lopez, and he'll come under pressure to say who was paying him to turn over Ullmann. So it has to look like they've just run into a border patrol by bad luck.

'I've got a couple of chaps who'll be togged up in an approximation to Paraguayan Army uniforms, but they can't form an entire military detachment on their own. We need an illusion that there are a lot more troops out there in the darkness. That's where you come in. At the operative moment, all you need to do is shoot off a lot of ammo into the darkness in roughly the right direction and leave the rest to us.'

'I don't need to hit anything.'

'You absolutely need to not hit anything, including me, but also my fake Paraguayan soldiers, Ullmann and the poor sod who runs the ferry and who is going to get the fright of his life.'

'So I shoot into the air?'

'Oh, no.' He smiled. 'It's going to be a lot more of a spectacle than that. Drink up, and I'll show you.'

They drove on for another hour, and then it was the turning to Villanova. The road was bare earth, and they had to slow down to save the car from a flat tyre or a broken spring. The journey became both hot and tedious, relieved only by the latent excitement about the ambush to come. He clearly didn't want to discuss it, and talking about anything else would be artificial, so she lapsed into silence.

Hal was scanning the fields to either side, and after a while found what he was looking for: an abandoned farm where they could prepare themselves for the night without being observed or overheard. He took a cart track up to the walls of the half-ruined farmhouse and parked out of sight. Then he opened the boot, took out their cases, rolled up the carpet and fiddled about for a few minutes, until with a heavy thud, something fell out from beneath the car. A moment later, he had retrieved a wide metal tube, about three feet long and six inches across and looking exactly like a car exhaust.

He rested it on the ground, felt for a catch, and then lifted open the top part. Inside, wrapped in oilskin, were a series of sausage-like packages. He began to withdraw their contents and lay them out on the ground. First came what looked like a pistol, except that the barrel was strangely wide, like a small cannon. There were a dozen chunky cartridges to go with it, each with a coloured band at one end.

Then he drew out a wicked-looking gun with a stubby barrel welded to a crude stock. She'd seen these before in every film about the French Resistance. Next to it he placed a row of spare magazines.

'Is that a Sten?'

'Actually, it's a Sterling SMG. A more refined cousin, but the same principle. Light, rugged, not very accurate, but by God it can make some noise. I'll show you how it works in a minute.'

There were more items in the treasure trove, some entirely mysterious, and some worryingly plain, including a little nest of six hand grenades. Just looking at them made her feel queasy. He placed them all out of sight in the car, except for the Sterling. He looked around carefully, but they were still alone, except for the line of trees along the distant road, the high grass that had already encroached on the fields, and the ever-present hum of cicadas.

'So, the Sterling. Safety catch here, trigger here. Shoots in three modes. Single, semi-automatic and fully automatic. You'll leave it in semi. Fires bursts of five shots at a time. Won't run out of rounds too quickly. OK?'

She nodded.

'Standard magazine. Takes nineteen rounds. Actually takes twenty, but let's not put too much strain on the spring. Don't want it to jam. I'll show you what to do if it does, but that would be tedious on the night.'

He taught her thoroughly, perhaps more so than she would have liked, with the sun beating down on them. She was shown how to strip and reassemble it, how to clean it, load it, unload it, and how to fit and remove the silencer that screwed onto the front of the barrel.

'Not that it's exactly silent, even with it on. And tonight, we'll want as much noise as possible. But for now, it makes it a little less likely anyone will come asking questions.'

At last, they went inside the ruined house. From one of the back windows they could see the wall of the barn about twenty feet away.

'We'll shoot at that. Being in here will keep the noise down, and we won't get ricochets whistling round our heads.'

Once the gun was in her hands, he was careful to stand behind her, his hands raised as if to grab it back.

'Aim for the bottom of the wall. It'll try and pull up. If you have your other hand here, that'll help keep the barrel down.'

He was standing behind her, his arms round her.

'Just a gentle squeeze.'

The noise was far louder than she'd expected, but

the gun did what she wanted. There were a couple of puffs in the dirt, and some chunks knocked out of the plaster.

'And again.'

She squeezed out a couple more bursts, each one a little more controlled, and was almost disappointed when the noise turned to a feeble clacking.

'You see how it eats the ammunition? Mix in a few single shots if you can.'

She nodded, sniffing the exotic scent of cordite smoke. For a moment, it had all been a lot of fun. Then she remembered what these toys could do to flesh and bone.

11

Dusk found them by the river, about five miles downstream of the ferry. They left the car out of sight and then Hal checked the equipment once more while she brewed up on their camping stove. Then they sat by the river, sipping their tea and watching their shadows lengthen, while Hal blew cigarette smoke into the sky to help keep the mosquitos away. The far shore was much like theirs: banks of red earth, a few scrubby bushes, trees, plenty of cover. Between, there was a hundred yards or more of river, heavy with silt.

After an age, they heard the low rumble of a heavy engine from down-river, out of sight around a long, lazy bend. Hal threw his cigarette away and waved as a launch came into sight, long and sleek, one man at the wheelhouse just back from the centre. He was wearing the usual short-sleeved white shirt, and there was no sign of anyone pretending to be military.

The launch pulled into the shore and two more men appeared. The extra one, it seemed, was the owner – or at least the guardian – of the launch, and had come along for the ride and to share in the money that Hal clearly possessed in abundance. Hal himself didn't seem too surprised by this, and after a bit of haggling agreed to pay a little more for the extra hand. There were smiles at this, and even more when one of the men produced a pile of green uniforms and they realised one of these was for the *chica*.

When she returned from changing behind the car, they laughed at the way the uniform engulfed her, even with the sleeves rolled up. But when Hal handed her the Sterling, and she cradled it naturally in her arms, they eyed it with envy and let the joke go.

Hal had explained to her that their cover was as agents of the Federal Government in Brasilia, more than a thousand miles to the north, which would account for their odd accents. Even so, she made a point of saying very little.

They climbed aboard and settled down in the front cabin. Now they were off, time seemed to move more quickly. She had to concentrate as Hal explained the plan over and over to the three Paraguayans and made them repeat it each time. She guessed it was to try and rein in their high spirits. They were not much more than boys, round-faced and smiling, and the half-criminal, half-patriotic role was having a lot more effect on them than the flask of local white rum they passed between themselves. But they held their rifles with a lot of competence. Hal had said they were hunters in their spare time and knew the river well.

The boat forged on against the current. Clemency pulled her belt a notch tighter and rolled up her sleeves again. The uniform was rough against her skin, as well as being too large, but it helped her believe in her role, and to feel part of Hal's unit.

His military experience was very obvious now. Waiting to go into action put a strain on the nerves, and he'd planned to fill this time with routine. The three of them were told to strip and clean their guns and pick through the ammunition to look for any round that might be less than perfect and risk causing a jam. She was told to empty each one of the magazines for the Sterling and do the same, and also to replace every third round with a special tracer bullet that would glow in the dark.

'If they fire back, you want to aim right over their heads. That'll give them something to think about, but there'll be no risk of anyone getting hurt.'

She'd only just finished this by the time the engine note dropped and they eased into the side of the river once more. Hal doused the cabin light and they let their eyes adjust to the dark. Coming onto the deck, she saw the rotten remains of a jetty beside them. She scrambled onto it, feeling the timbers give a little beneath her, and hurried onto solid land. The night was clear and in the starlight she could make out a stand of trees and a broken-down shack, saplings growing through what remained of the roof.

A final check, final instructions. The launch, it turned out, was to wait there for Hal's signal. Settling her absurd cap on her head, she followed him along the path that edged the river bank, watching out for fallen branches and hoping that they weren't themselves walking into a trap. As he'd said on the first day they'd met, the Paraguayan border was a long way from Buenos Aires, let alone London. What would she do if anything happened to Hal? She had no papers, no money, no proper clothes, no real idea of where she was. All she had was trust that he knew what he was doing and would look after her.

She moved slowly, carefully, following his example. Though it was hot enough and steamy enough to be in the jungle – she was sweating and wished she had a bottle of water – there was none of the noise she associated with the jungle at night. It could have been a walk though the English countryside – a faint breeze rustling the trees, the flow of the water sensed more than heard, and occasionally the sound of an animal snorting or moving out of their way.

At last there was a light ahead, and the sound of a radio playing tinny music. They crept on until the single-story house was in sight. An old man, with a short, grizzled beard and the bent, awkward movements of a man suffering from rheumatism, was pottering around on the veranda. There was enough light from his lantern to show the boat, tied up to a landing stage that extended twenty feet from the bank.

Hal gestured to her to show that this was where she was to wait for his signal, and then, with a last pat on her shoulder, he glided into the dark.

She glanced at her watch. It was a few minutes short of eleven o'clock, and Hal had said that it wasn't likely that Ullmann would be there until at least two in the morning.

She sat quietly for a while, then began cautiously to explore the space around her. There was the tree, the path, the little patch of reeds that fringed the river. When she had felt her way around, and was confident she couldn't be seen, and wouldn't trip or make a noise, she could then move about with confidence, keeping herself alert and working off some of the tension.

Still the time passed slowly. The splash of a bird on the river was an event. She envied the boys in the launch, no doubt playing cards or chatting. She could have done with some of their *caña*. The one thing she refused to do was to look at her watch. That would drive her mad, because it was bound to be longer left to wait than she could possibly imagine. Better to sit quietly for as long as she could, and then, when she could not bear to wait any longer, find relief in movement – even if it were only retying the laces on her boots.

By now, the old man had finished checking through his nets and had gone inside. The radio was off, though there was still the faint glow of the lantern. Perhaps making himself tea, she thought, and was at once gripped by thirst.

Then came the sound of a car, labouring in low gear; no, two cars. Their headlights caught the tops of the trees by the river, dipped out of sight again. She reached hurriedly for her gun and slipped off the safety catch.

The old man came outside again, listening, clearly puzzled. He was still standing there when two cars pulled up in front of him, between the shack and the river.

Two men got out of the first car, heavily built and wearing jackets, despite the heat. From behind, Ullmann came forward to join them. There was some explanation, and Clemency caught some of the words, about how they were running later than they expected and were sorry to disturb him. But this didn't cover the tension that she could feel even from fifty feet away.

The man, whatever he thought of it all, took the money and led them down to the bank of the river. They began to pile up their luggage: several suitcases, a couple of trunks, a kit bag and – strange choice for an emergency escape – a pair of tennis rackets.

The old man picked up the first suitcase and began to carry it to the boat.

Then, like a firework, there was a burst of light

above them, a flare soaring into the sky and arcing towards the far bank. It turned the river to a vile green-silver, and the group by the boat looked up as one, their faces wearing a sickly pallor.

Then a shout, telling them to raise their hands.

One of the men grabbed Ullmann by the arm and hurried him towards the boat. The other drew a gun and looked around him.

The voice – Hal's voice – called a warning. But they ignored it, pushing the old man into the boat, getting him to start the motor.

Then the first shot.

Ullmann had run back, as if to pick up one of the bags. Now he hesitated. Another shot hit the wooden landing stage a few feet away from him, sending splinters flying.

The man with the gun had taken shelter by the side of the house. He began to fire into the trees, away from Clemency. The guard in the boat joined in.

From behind, downstream, Clemency heard the pulse of the launch's engine. A strong beam of light began to probe the sky. She remembered she was not just a spectator. Standing braced against the tree, she fired over the heads of the group crouched in the boat. The first burst went wildly into the sky. The second was just right, looping into the far bank.

The man by the house ran for it, firing at her. One of the bullets scattered the leaves above her head, but she didn't feel any fear. She calmly put another burst into the river a few yards from the ferry.

They had the engine going now and were pulling away from the bank. Ullmann had a pistol in his hand, pointing at the old ferryman – but he clearly needed no encouragement to get away from the fight.

The two guards were still on the bank, firing blind into the trees around them. She had to admire their courage. In the light from the house, they were sitting targets.

She glanced over to the ferry. Already it was in the middle of the river, and almost lost to sight in the dark. The launch was still out of sight, though its spotlight was probing the night, and there was a chance the ferry would get away.

Now one of the gunmen had reached the house and put out the lantern. She remembered Hal telling her that she should fire and then move, so her position wasn't marked down.

She sent another stream of bullets over the roof of the house, thinking how pretty the coloured tracer was in the dark. Then she ran twenty yards back along the path, and ducked down to the very edge of the river.

There was a car now on the far bank, and two men standing watching, dark against the starlit sky. The ferry was nearly over, and still the launch was too far off to do anything except shout confused orders that the ferryman ignored.

She changed the magazine, desperate to know what to do. From where she was, she was confident she could hit the ferry. The thought of Ullmann escaping made her burn with rage. But what would Hal want her to do?

In the end, the thought of the old man, just as likely to be killed as Ullmann, tipped the balance. She fired as close to the ferry as she dared, and Ullmann ducked suddenly. The boat tipped and he fell over the side, floundering in the shallow water. He struggled to the bank, and two men came down to help him to his feet and hurry him to the waiting car.

Another flare soared into the sky as the car on the far bank slid round and made off into the night. And then Clemency realised that she'd heard the other cars do the same a few moments before – no doubt the drivers and the two bodyguards making their escape.

It was over. Now the launch appeared and came alongside the jetty. She walked down the path as Hal emerged from the undergrowth, grinning widely. He went to the baggage piled by the edge of the river and began to examine it. He looked up as she approached.

'That stirred 'em up, eh?'

'He got away. Should I have shot him?'

'God, no. That would have caused one hell of a stink.' He had picked up an attaché case that Ullmann had abandoned and was talking with only part of his mind engaged. 'The whole point was for no-one to get hurt.'

'He got away.'

'For now. But we've smashed his operation over here. Capturing him would have been jam on top, but let's not be greedy, eh? Ramón! Julio!'

He switched into Spanish to summon the Paraguayans, and directed them to take all the luggage on board. Almost at once they cast off and the launch began to swing round in the current, until it pointed south again.

On the bank, the ferryman was looking at them nervously.

'Tell him to be more careful who he takes on his ferry next time,' Hal said to the man at the wheel, who shouted it across the water with great delight. Then the engine gunned and they were on their way. The launch had its lights on now and their uniforms would show up clearly, particularly the distinctive caps. Perhaps that's what Hal wanted. Certainly, he seemed in great good humour for a man whose quarry had slipped through his fingers.

She went into the cabin, where Hal and his men were talking excitedly, reliving the firefight, laughing at every chance. She was suddenly very tired, but remembered she should strip and clean the gun. When he saw her, Hal said something about her being the only soldier amongst them, which amused them hugely, and they passed her the bottle of *caña*. It was even more blistering than she had expected. She coughed and gasped, but they only laughed all the more.

The gun cleaned and reassembled, she sat on one of the benches and rested her eyes for a moment, only to be woken much later, stiff and stupid with sleep as she was helped onto the bank. Hal was parting from their three comrades with many serious protestations of mutual admiration, and then the launch was away. There were some heavy splashes and Clemency looked at him questioningly.

'Ullmann's luggage. I went through it all on the way back. I've kept his private papers. Quite a good haul.'

Yet she sensed disappointment, as if he'd hoped for more. Perhaps the adrenalin was wearing off, and Ullmann's escape was sinking in.

12

He didn't say so, but Clemency was sure that Hal was pleased with her. For one thing, he took her with him when he went to meet Captain Lopez and drive out together to Ullmann's *estancia*. True, he had told her to keep in the background and not say anything beyond hello and goodbye, but at least she was part of the team.

Captain Lopez was all smiles with Hal, and gallantry with Clemency, and seemed very pleased with life – as well he might, given how he had been paid handsomely for doing what he wanted to do anyway. Here at least was one Brazilian who didn't think Ullmann's crimes were of less importance for having been committed thousands of miles away, or years ago.

'You say he went into the river?' he said when Hal had finished his account of the evening. 'That I wished I had seen.'

'He left his luggage behind. There were a few papers I thought you might like to have.'

Hal passed over a heavy folder. Lopez rested it in his lap and began to scan through it, occasionally glancing up to make sure he was still on the road.

'Aha!' he said after a while. 'Montez! I wondered where he got his money.'

He flicked on, then leaned over and dropped it onto

the back seat, winking at Clemency as he did so.

'I think this will keep me busy for some time. Ah, here we are.'

He turned off on the track that led to the Ullmann estate. After a few minutes, the house came into sight. There were still a couple of police vehicles, and also two very battered lorries, with what looked like a whole family, from grandmother to toddler, looking out of the back of the nearest one as they approached.

'Who's the audience?' Hal asked, smiling, but with an edge to his voice.

'A refinement,' Lopez said. 'When we have finished searching, there is a chance that these people will loot it. And perhaps set fire to it. You know what the criminal classes are like in every country.'

'I do. A nice touch.'

'There may be questions about the actions of the police,' Lopez said innocently. 'But we cannot be everywhere.'

He led them at pace into the house, past the heavy oak furniture, the carpets and porcelain, the paintings and books. Hal had explained that they would only have an hour or so to search the house. After that, the police would have to start to take down their roadblocks, and there was a chance that someone from the Link would arrive to tidy up any loose ends.

'My men have made a start,' Lopez said, throwing open the doors to Ullmann's study. Inside, it was as if a whirlwind with a malicious intelligence had been at work. It looked like chaos, with the books flung out of their cases, the pictures stripped from the walls, the rugs rolled back and half the floorboards up. But there was method to it – like the rows of holes drilled in the plaster to find if there was a safe hidden there. There were papers piled on every surface, and now it was their chance to go through them.

'Don't spend any time reading the stuff,' Hal said. 'If it looks at all interesting, throw it in one of these sacks. Everything else, just chuck it in a corner.'

She started at once, conscious how little time they had. But working in the registry in Bern gave her an instinctive feel for what files mattered and what could be safely cast aside. A lot of the paperwork was apparently routine, mainly about the widows and children of departed *kamerads*, right down to paying for school fees or house repairs. The Link began to look a lot like a friendly society, committed to looking after its members in times of hardship, and what could be better cover than that? But there were enough hints in the documents passing through her hands to show there was a mailed fist within this velvet glove of good-fellowship. The donations to the election campaigns of the main political parties were lavish enough to buy plenty of protection.

'What chance is there of getting Ullmann extradited from Paraguay?' she asked.

'Precisely none,' Hal said cheerfully. 'Don't worry about him escaping. It's intelligence about his organisation that we're after.'

But it didn't seem like that. Hal attacked the mountains of files not as if he wanted to build a picture of the enemy, but as if there were a single document that he was after.

'But why? What's this really about?'

He didn't tell her it was beyond top secret, or that keeping her in ignorance was for her own safety. He simply ignored her.

She kept on working, glancing at bank statements

and letters to lawyers, receipted airline tickets and title deeds. The cream of Ullmann's archive might be elsewhere – the lists of active members, the minutes of their innermost councils – but there was plenty here to use to reconstruct how their organisation worked and what its aims were, if someone – or a team of someones – had the time to work on it.

'Maybe we could use some of this to exchange for more of what Cristina Navarra has,' she suggested.

'What? Oh, yes,' he said casually. 'We'll need to get it back to BA first. Catsmeat will have first dibs on it. Maybe he'll think it worth throwing her some scraps.'

His contemptuous tone stung her. It was as if he wanted her to know that she was a fool to think that a local lawyer would have anything worthwhile; that both women should know their place. Perhaps the file on the murderer of the RAF pilots had turned out to be a bust. In silence, she doggedly worked on her task until Captain Lopez came to tell them that their time was up.

They carried the bags of documents out to Hal's car and they filled the boot and most of the back seat. She wondered what they would do when they came to the border, but Hal already had that planned out. He'd arranged to have it all shipped direct to Buenos Aires, from where it could go in the diplomatic bag back to London for analysis.

'We'll be completely clean, apart from the arsenal in the false exhaust. I don't want to be parted from that. We've given the Link a bloody nose, you and I, and they'll want to hit back.'

She was absurdly pleased that he included her in their success, and her sulky mood slipped away. They parted from Captain Lopez with the same kind of mutual esteem they'd shared with their private army of the night before, and as they drove off Clemency asked how much this had all cost.

'Including Lopez? About two thousand sterling. Pretty good value, I think. We'll see what London says when they get all that bumf. Funny thing is, I don't think Lopez is making much out of it. He has lots of people of his own to pay for. He's just a decent chap. Or maybe the Link will be more generous to him for tipping Ullmann off about the raid.'

'Will he tell them about you? About us?'

Hal looked surprised.

'I doubt it, but I suppose he might. Or they might just put two and two together. I suppose we'll find out when we get back to BA. If someone starts taking pot shots at us, then we'll need to find a new cover story.'

They were back on the main road and heading south towards Ponto Porã and the Paraguay border. As usual, there wasn't much traffic, and most of it was carts or trucks. When a dark Mercedes sped by in the other direction, Hal speculated, half-jokingly, that it might be members of the Link heading to the *Casa Anna*.

'They're bound to send someone, aren't they? He said. 'Except they're about three hours too late. And… yes!'

Surprised by this exclamation of great satisfaction, she turned to him, and saw his eyes fixed on the rear-view mirror. She squirmed around in her seat. They were at least five miles from the *estancia*, but she could still see clearly a plume of black smoke rising into the blue sky.

'That's thrown down the gauntlet,' Hal said. 'Now we'll see what comes.'

13

They drove through the night and reached Buenos Aires the following afternoon, going straight to the Embassy to brief Pryce-Jones. During their brief stops, Hal had dictated a report to Clemency and he had this on his knee as he spoke. Pryce-Jones said very little until Hal had finished. Then he sat back, his fingers placed together to form a steeple.

'Do you think Ullmann will work out that you were behind this?'

'Perhaps. We came across Braun, who's reputed to be their head of counter-intelligence, and he's supposed to be pretty smart. He's bound to connect this to our searches in the archives. Luckily there's no need for us to go back in. I expect he'll go over everything leading up to the raid on Ullmann's place and he'll certainly wonder if this mysterious Englishman might have something to do with it. Or he might take Route One and bribe the police chief.'

'And then? Might this secret service of theirs – the Link or *Wachhund* or ODESSA or whatever it calls itself this week – might they act against you here is Buenos Aires?'

'Most likely he'll think we're police, and he'll know that killing a policeman is a sure way to bring the whole lot of them down on your heads. Obviously he'd warn off everyone in the Link from having anything to do with us, starting with Werner. There is a chance he'll do something more extreme. That's a risk we'll have to take.'

For the first time, Pryce-Jones turned to Clemency.

'And you, Miss White? Are you content to take that risk?'

'What would they do?' she asked.

'It's hard to tell,' Hal said. 'Kidnap. Assassination. Kidnap is more likely because they'd want to know what I know before disposing of me. But that kind of thing takes time to arrange. That's why we need to move quickly against Werner. The longer we wait, the more chance of them putting two and two together, and the more time for them to cook up something nasty.'

It was odd to hear Hal talking about his own death in this way. It reminded her of a time when she'd had a boyfriend, Rory, who'd loved mountaineering. He and his friends would discuss a climb they planned for the next day with just this same dispassionate analysis of the risks. This was a comfort, for as far as she knew, Rory was still alive.

'We need to get inside his house,' Pryce-Jones said. 'Hal, you'll need to give your contact a kick and find a day when the place is empty. Also, we need to know the layout. Miss White can arrange an invitation through his daughter, I'm sure. When can you next see her?'

'I'll call her this evening and say I'm back. So hopefully tomorrow.'

'Good. What would be more natural than asking to look over the house? You can make a floor plan afterwards.'

'Shall I start to pull a team together?' Hal asked. 'Driver, lookout and so on?'

'I'm not so sure,' Pryce-Jones said, his eyes on the ceiling as he considered this, more than ever the Oxford don. 'The more people in the know, the greater the risk of a leak. After all, if the Link are as good as we think they might be, they'll be looking for a way to penetrate our operation. Perhaps using an intermediary.'

Clemency was used to the way they talked as if she weren't really there – as if she were a servant, trusted not to repeat anything she heard, but having nothing to contribute of her own. But more than ever she felt they were saying something to each other beyond mere words.

'What about the Soviets?' Hal asked.

'I think you might be right that they're sniffing around. The Y intercepts suggest extra traffic in the GRU code, though of course we can't read it. I've set up a dinner party for Friday night and invited Maliakov along. As you said, it's a chance for you to get the measure of the man and also see if he takes a particular interest in you.'

'Who is Maliakov?' Clemency asked.

'The GRU resident here. His cover is cultural attaché. The excuse for dragging him along to dinner is that he has some Russian scribbler called Sorokin over on a lecture tour. Otherwise, we're not aware of any new faces at the Soviet Bloc embassies, so either Maliakov is recruiting local talent or he only has a watching brief for now.'

'And we stay at the hotel for now?'

'It would be a pity to drop your cover,' Pryce-Jones replied. 'We've got a safe house lined up if we need it. What do you think?'

'The amount I'm paying the deputy manager to

report anything suspicious, we should be safer than the crown jewels. But you never know.'

'Let's review that after the dinner on Friday. Now, Miss White, could you type up Mr Linklater's report for me? I'll use it as the basis for the telegram to London. You'll find a typewriter in the room opposite, and you shouldn't be disturbed.'

'Of course.'

Hal handed her the notes and she left the room, closing the door softly behind her, like a good secretary. But she was aware of a change in mood. The two men would be able to speak more openly in her absence. This was why she had been dismissed.

She wondered what it was they wanted to keep from her.

◊

On her way back to the hotel, Clemency realised how relieved she was not to be going back to the archive that night. She had no desire to fall into the hands of the Link. But in abandoning the search, Hal and Pryce-Jones weren't thinking of her safety. There must be another reason why Zoll was now of less interest.

'Who is Dr Zoll?' she asked impulsively. 'I've seen Ullmann, and I know about Werner, but I've got no idea about Zoll. Was he a really medical doctor? What did he actually do? And why is he the one who's hardest to trace?'

Hal paused before replying, not taking his eyes from the road.

'Zoll is a doctor twice over. Medicine and physics. Very clever chap, by all accounts. Saw action at the end of the first world war, then combined medical studies with being in one of the *Freikorps* that fought the Communists. He drifted into the Nazi Party early on, and also made a switch to physics. Worked on a Luftwaffe project for most of the war, then went into hiding like the rest. If I'd been him I'd have made sure I stayed hard to find too. In '43 he was attached to one of the death camps and began experimenting on the prisoners. Men, women, children. At least 500 of them. Most of them died the most horrible, lingering death you could imagine, like a mix of being poisoned and burned alive. Those few that did survive were taken away and executed.'

'And the Argentinians let him in?'

'He had skills they wanted. Dr Zoll was also a good Catholic, and more importantly, a good anti-Communist, so the Vatican helped hide him until '47 and then gave him a new identity. Oh, don't look too shocked. They did this on an industrial scale. They had a whole team of Vatican officials working on it. Catsmeat slightly played that down – he's very High Anglican and so is twitchy about anything knocking Rome – but without the Vatican, most of these Nazis would have been rounded up.'

'But why do we want him now?'

The shutters came down.

'That, I cannot tell you.'

◊

Clemency had been puzzling about how to engineer an invite to Petra's house. In the event, she needn't have worried, as there was a note from Petra waiting for her asking her to call as soon as she was back in BA. She went for morning coffee and stayed for lunch, for Petra wanted to hear every detail of her trip and then was immersed in plans to ensure that Hal settled on Argentina for their new life, and was not seduced by Brazil or Paraguay.

'You need a place to escape from the countryside,' Petra had insisted. 'A place with culture. Art. Opera. Proper shops. Did you visit Asunción? There is nothing there. Nothing. And Rio is too far. You will never go. It has to be Buenos Aires.'

Petra was more than happy to show her over the house, rattling on about the best way to design a larder, or organise a kitchen, or stop keep a cellar dry and free from mustiness. Nothing was kept from Clemency – not even her father's study, where she even insisted on showing her the safe, hidden behind a picture, and saying it was an essential if Clemency was not going to be parted from her jewellery.

'If it is in a bank, you will never see it,' Petra said with feeling, though she hardly wore any jewellery herself, preferring the simple, scrubbed look of an Alpine milkmaid. It made Clemency wonder why Petra would think of her as someone who owned jewellery of the kind you had to keep in a safe. Perhaps her imitation of a daughter of the English aristocracy was better than she had thought.

She caught a tram back into town and sketched the layout of the house on her way, and then turned it into a clear plan, to scale, in her hotel room, enjoying the task so much she found herself adding little flourishes and taking pains over the labels – sash window, bolt top and bottom – as she leaned over, her tongue between her teeth, just like at school.

None of it felt like a betrayal of her new friend.

The enormity of what her father had done made such thoughts ridiculous. But still the strain of the day caught up with her during her tango lesson that evening, where she struggled to concentrate, and Lucia's tongue became more and more acid.

'You spend some days in the country and you come back a peasant. Can you only dance a *schottische* now? A polka?'

It was a relief when the lesson came to an end. Lucia went to fetch some tea and Clemency was discretely flapping her blouse to try and cool down when Cristina Navarra arrived. As before, Lucia greeted her friend warmly, then made herself absent. Cristina, torn between wanting to tell the English what she knew, and wanting something back in return, produced a thin folder for Clemency to take back to Hal.

'I understand you have travelled to Entre Ríos and Misiones? These are good places to look. There were strong German colonies long before the war, and the Federal Government does not interfere there too much. There is the border with Brazil and with Paraguay which goes for thousands of kilometres. With a boat, you can cross anywhere. Did you see the border?'

'Yes.'

'Then you know. If things are difficult in one country, how easy to take a holiday somewhere more pleasant for a while.'

'I can imagine.'

'But the truth is still here in Buenos Aires. Always, we must follow the money. Even before the war ends, the Nazis are buying companies here. They said it was to facilitate trade and to get round the blockade of the Allies, but millions of pesos came this way. They used this to buy legitimate businesses, often using

Argentinians as the directors so they could not easily be traced. It has taken many years to follow these trails. We have built up a very considerable archive. It may be possible to arrange for Sir Linklater, your most elusive friend, to see these papers.'

'I'm sure he'd want to do that,' Clemency replied loyally, though she doubted it. He had shown no interest in the lists of possible Nazi sympathisers she had worked so hard to compile in the archive.

'But he is so busy,' Cristina sympathised. 'Perhaps a sample will help to convince him to change his arrangement and make time to see me. Why do you not choose one of these to take to him?'

Clemency opened the folder. There were eight single sheets of paper, each one typed up neatly but with no heading to the paper, no signature. They were a little like CVs, in that there was a name and address at the top of each and a series of roles they had filled – directorships, mainly, of a range of businesses, listed year by year. It wasn't hard to know which to pick, for the fifth one down was Reinhard Rausch.

Then Clemency saw that it was a trap. She had stopped going through the papers, giving away her interest in Rausch. She looked up and saw a hint of triumph in the lawyer's eyes.

◊

Back at the hotel, Clemency had the evening to herself, while Hal was off on a mysterious errand. But she couldn't shake free from the feeling that she had blundered badly with Cristina. As much as she was fed up with Hal not trusting her, even to the extent of not saying where he went at night, she also had to admit he might have a point in keeping her in the dark. The more she knew, the more chance of giving something away.

This wasn't the only way in which she felt churned up by her meeting with Cristina. As she left, the lawyer had pressed another file on her, much more bulky. In it were photostats of witness statements she had gathered to use against some of the Nazis hiding in plain sight in Argentina. Clemency had leafed through these casually, and then realised that this was testimony from survivors of the concentration camps. The little she had read had sickened her, and she had put it aside.

It lay now on the bed, and even with the buff cover closed and tied up with tape, it was demanding of her the same question she had been asking from the day she arrived in Argentina. Why were they hunting these three men?

Was it to bring them to justice? Then why be so casual with the evidence they had gathered from the *estancia?* It had arrived in a series of chests at the Embassy, but these remained unopened. And why be so uninterested in taking what Cristina had to offer?

Nothing that either Hal or Pryce-Jones had said or done made her think they cared particularly about the murder of six million Jewish people, or the other atrocities the Nazis had carried out. Even the file on the murdered prisoners had been ignored.

So why were they there?

Up to now, she had pushed her doubts aside. But she couldn't ignore the voices in the file. She owed it to them to read the file, wherever it might take her.

14

Pryce-Jones lived in a large detached house close to the Bosques de Palermo, down a winding lane where grand houses stood half-hidden behind high walls and jacaranda trees. A white-coated steward escorted them to a large drawing room where the other guests were already assembled. At once a tall, fair woman who turned out to be Pryce-Jones's wife Venetia came over, trailing chiffon, her welcome a little too much for comfort.

Although the greeting rang false, Clemency did not hold it against her. Diplomat's wives had to live through their husbands. As they often had more ability and drive, it was not surprising when they started to take it all too seriously. Better that than drink or affairs. And to be married to Pryce-Jones must be a trial to drive any woman to the edge of madness, let alone some social insincerity.

For a few minutes, Clemency was given her full and flattering attention – what Peter had called 'the full *Führerkontakt*' when practiced by the wife of their Ambassador in Bern. Venetia informed her about the most important aspects of her new life in Argentina, about accommodation, servants, how to deal with local bureaucrats. Like Petra, she told Clemency that she had to have a base in Buenos Aires to avoid sinking into the soil and turning vegetable – there was simply no culture outside the capital, with the possible exception of the second city of Córdoba. Then there were instructions about schooling and choosing the right nanny, and here Venetia became briefly human. Perhaps her children were some compensation for her husband.

Dinner was announced and they went through to the dining room and Clemency was introduced to Maliakov, the GRU man whose cover was cultural attaché. Was she imagining it, or was his smile of greeting ironic, as if he knew exactly who she was, and why she was here? Perhaps more than she understood herself?

They exchanged some words about how she was enjoying Buenos Aires, and she was struck by the coldness in his expression. She thought of Peter, surrounded by men like this, and she had to blink away a tear, pretending she had something in her eye. Yet his presence was also a blessing. Hal and Pryce-Jones would spend their evening sparring with him, trying to learn more than they gave away. This would leave her free for some espionage of her own – if, when it came to it, she dared to put her plan into action.

Even so, she was relieved to find herself seated at the far end of the table from Maliakov, next to the writer Sorokin. He bowed as she took her seat.

'It is a great pleasure to meet you, Miss Black. But also I must apologise.'

'Whatever for?'

'That you must spend the evening in my company, when you could have enjoyed a little flirting with one of the many most handsome young men at our table.'

She glanced around. It was true that there were two or three rather self-consciously attractive youths, all

intense eyes and chiselled cheekbones. She wondered
how they fitted in.

'I'm engaged.'

'Yes, but not seriously,' Sorokin said in an offhand
way. 'Not for love. Your fiancé is an admirable man
and I am sure will go far in his profession, but he is
not the love of your life.'

Sorokin was smiling, but also watching her closely.
Perhaps he'd already sensed the businesslike character
of their relationship.

'Tell me about your books,' she said, to distract him.

'Ah, you understand that we writers are only happy
when talking about our work.'

'Would I have seen any of them in English?'

'Alas, no. The demand for these amusements is so
very different in my country than in yours. In some
ways it is most difficult to write novels of espionage
at all.'

'Is it a sensitive matter?' she asked, glancing
down the table to where the GRU man was deep in
conversation with Pryce-Jones.

'Oh no,' Sorokin replied with a laugh. 'I can write
what I wish. My government has no concerns. It is
more a matter of the taste of the people. They do not
care much for spies. The Western examples do not
help, with your Matt Helm and your James Bond.
This procession of boring heroes. All so much the
same with their guns and gadgets and martial arts.
You think this is how real spies are?'

'I don't know.'

'Believe me, this is not the true world of espionage.
But of course, these books, and now all these films,
they are about something else entirely.'

She looked at him enquiringly.

'Sex. That is their true subject. Think of who reads them. The worker travelling home. The tired executive on the aeroplane. His life is dull. He is working too hard. His wife maybe loves him less. But the hero of the book, he can save the world and sleep with all the girls. This is why they are so popular in the West. They are a cure for the impotence of modern Western man.'

'What about women?' she asked, as her role seemed to be to feed Sorokin his lines.

'You mean, what need does it meet for them? A good question. For most, it is the tall dark handsome stranger of tradition who sweeps them to his bed and so proves she is desirable. For some, maybe, the excitement of the locations, the danger. That, I am sure, is you. For others, it will be the thrill of imagining themselves the villainess – so beautiful, so deadly.

'But most women, they are married and they worry if their husband is straying. Girls, they are now everywhere. Secretaries. Typists. Clerks. Maybe even doctors and lawyers. It is no longer a man's world at work. For the men, this is fuel for their dreams, but for their wives, there is much to fear. When he says he is working late, is he perhaps at dinner with his secretary? When he goes away for business, who else is in his hotel room? You see?'

'What does—'

But Sorokin was caught up in his own cleverness.

'That is why the Western spy must so often have a girl agent with him. She takes the place of the wife. Keeping him from temptation. Picture the scene. We have seen it a hundred times. He returns to his hotel room. There is a girl as beautiful as she is evil, waiting to seduce him. She wears very little. They kiss. They embrace. She raises the knife behind his back, ready to plunge it into him. A shot, and she falls dead at his feet. Who has shot her? His female assistant. She pulls a face, he shrugs his shoulders. And with a sigh of regret, he steps over the body of the dead girl and returns to his mission.'

He finished with his hands open wide, to prove how right he was.

'I didn't follow what you said about impotence.'

He took a deep draught of his wine.

'When I use that term, I am thinking of the national spirit. America is in decline. In engineering, in atomic power, in space, it is the Soviet Union that leads. As a nation, America is becoming impotent. England also. So the people want books that show they still powerful.

'We have nothing like this in the Soviet Union. There are no books and films with evil Americans trying to take over the world, or English sadists torturing women or planning to kill millions of people. What other explanation do you have? It must be impotence.'

Seminov produced this with triumph, just as the conversation around the table fell away, leaving *impotence* hanging in the air. The lull allowed Venetia to catch Clemency's eye to summon her from the room, leaving the men to their port and brandy. Surprised the dinner had passed so quickly, she followed her hostess into a rather bleak drawing room. Venetia hastily tidied away some stray school books.

'I know it must seem a little fanciful for the two of us to leave the gentlemen when it's only an informal supper but Jacob doesn't like it if we change the arrangements.'

It made Pryce-Jones sound like a child that was pleasant enough when he got his own way, but ready to make everyone else's life a misery when he was thwarted.

'Do you have to entertain a lot?' Clemency asked.

'Most evenings. Jacob believes it's his responsibility to keep connected. It's a little hard on the children, of course.'

'If you'd like to see them now, I can amuse myself with a magazine,' Clemency suggested, and Venetia needed little persuasion.

'Clara is a wonderful nanny,' she said, pausing at the doorway, 'but I don't like to miss wishing them good night.'

Clemency waited a few moments, then made her way into the hall. The drawing room and dining room she knew already, which left three more doors. Thinking wouldn't help, so she opened the nearest. In front of her was a closet packed with riding coats and boots, skis and scarves, tennis racquets and oilskin coats and at the back, a heavy wooden box, like a young coffin, that held a croquet set.

'Lost?'

She spun round to find Pryce-Jones looking at her enquiringly. Once more she marvelled at his ability to be so outwardly courteous while making her feel such a fool. He opened the door to the lavatory and held it for her, and he was both the perfect host and a jailor returning her to her cell. She sat on the lid of the toilet and listened until his footsteps had returned to the dining room. Then she moved quickly across the hall and walked straight into what must be his study.

An overly large desk, with too much green leather. Heavy wooden chairs with seats in the same colour.

Weighty books on the shelves. Prints of Oxford colleges, eighteenth century farm animals, hunting scenes, and an oar above the fireplace. Apart from Pryce-Jones the Rower, it was all exactly as she had imagined, but all slightly off-key, as if done for effect, as if Pryce-Jones was not quite the younger son of the landed gentry he set himself up to be. It was too precise, too right, too much like a museum or a stage set.

These thoughts came in an instant. She was already at the desk, quietly opening each draw in turn, but they held only stationery. A glance through the desk diary. Nothing but times, names and occasional cryptic remarks. The files on the desk next, but they were about a reorganisation of the Embassy Registry. For a moment she was back in her old life in Bern, where such a document would have been of overwhelming interest.

Her foot came up against a bag sitting unseen beside the desk. A briefcase, invitingly open. She'd promised herself no more than five minutes, but she was loath to go away empty-handed.

Four slim files. Three were in the pre-printed buff format of a registry file, the kind she'd handled every day, that were official and recorded and available for anyone with the right security clearance. The fourth was plain. This would be the one.

She crouched down behind the desk and began to work her way through it, no more than a few seconds a page, relying on impressions more than reading the words. Phrases leapt from the pages. *Authorised expenditure… all necessary steps to recover the Covenant… immense damage to HMG's international reputation…* She read on, feeling the knowledge pumping into her like a drug being injected into her veins. The more she knew, the more dangerous the knowledge.

She slipped the file back into the case, wishing she'd been more careful to memorise its exact position. But there was no time to fret. She was already at the door and easing it open, just in time to catch a glimpse of Venetia hurrying guiltily down the stairs and into the drawing room. Clemency hurried to join her before Venetia had done more than look around in puzzlement for her guest, and then instinctively check that the coffee pot was hot.

A moment later, the door behind her opened and Pryce-Jones came in, leading in the men.

'Here we are,' he said genially. 'I hope you've enjoyed your chat.'

Venetia and Clemency, partners in crimes, if of different kinds, were quick to agree that they had.

15

The other guests had gone. Pryce-Jones had signalled to Hal that they should remain behind, and to Venetia that she should disappear, and now they were in his study, with whisky for the men and then, as an afterthought, the offer of a liqueur for Clemency that she was expected to turn down.

'Werner,' Pryce-Jones said, once they were settled. 'Tomorrow?'

'We're ready,' Hal replied, and Clemency wondered what it was they were ready to do, and what role she would be asked to play. All at the last minute, of course. But now she knew why she was being kept in the dark, and that it was nothing to do with security.

'We have established,' Pryce-Jones began, 'that Werner will be at a dinner celebrating ninety years of the Argentinian-German Fellowship tomorrow evening. We have a plan of his house, courtesy of Miss White. We have the make of the safe, and the sequence for opening it without the code.'

'How does that work?' Hal asked.

'The safe can be set to any one of five million codes, through a combination of numbers and turns to the left and right. But for every safe the manufacturer includes a sequence that will open the safe again, in case the combination is ever mis-set or forgotten. The postern code, they call it. The manufacturer happens to be a British firm, one of my colleagues had a chat with them and the code arrived by telegram earlier today. 54-36-90-4. All Miss White will have to do is enter it in the usual way and the thing will open. No more than ten seconds, I should think.'

'What will I find there?'

There was so much more she could have said, beginning with why they had lied to her about what the mission was about, and perhaps finishing with telling them that if they wanted the safe opened, they could do it themselves. But to do so would reveal that she had been turning her skills as a thief not against the enemy but against her own side.

'Bring all the papers you can get,' Hal said to her. 'From the desk as well. Don't bother trying to make it look like a burglary. Just in and out. I'll be waiting in the car in the next street.'

'Is there anything in particular I should look out for?' she asked. The two men exchanged a brief glance.

'There is one document in which we are particularly interested.' Pryce-Jones replied cautiously. 'I would expect it to be typed on heavy paper, about ten pages in length and bound in maroon leather boards. Foolscap in size. Whatever you do, don't leave it behind.'

This would be the Covenant, the document they were pursuing, the whole reason for the mission; but she had to play ignorant.

'What is it?'

'Don't worry about that,' Pryce-Jones said. 'You'll know it when you see it.'

◊

During the drive back to their hotel, they had their first row, just as if they were really engaged.

'Why can't I know what's going on?' she protested. 'I'm not blaming you,' she went on, though she was. 'I know it's Pryce-Jones. I've shown I can be trusted, haven't I?'

'It's not about trust,' he snapped. 'It's about doing your job. The way you go on about this just proves the point. You don't need to know, and that's the end of it.'

She stared out of the window at the passing streets, dark and deserted. Her mind kept returning to the folder she'd found in Pryce-Jones' study, so she changed the subject.

'What did you make of Maliakov?' she asked. 'Does he suspect you?'

'He's a professional,' Hal replied. 'You could never be sure what he knows or what he's thinking. We've got to assume he's interested in me.'

Interested in the Covenant, she guessed. That put things in a different light. She'd do anything to find it, and keep it hidden from the Soviets, if it thwarted their plans. The file she'd read had talked of damage to Britain's reputation. Maybe she was being too hard on Hal, too idealistic, to think only of righting the wrongs of the past, when there were such ruthless enemies surrounding her country here and now. And here was Hal, prepared to take on both the Nazis and the Soviets.

But her renewed warmth towards him didn't last long.

'You were quite a hit with that writer chap,' he said, just a little extra drawl to his voice. 'You were all over each other. Eyes for no-one else.'

'Nonsense.'

'Letting a Russian flirt with you one minute, and then complaining about not being told every secret the next. Pryce-Jones wasn't impressed, you know.'

She cursed Pryce-Jones under her breath, then fumed in silence all the way back to the hotel, and all the way to her room.

◊

If she were to be a professional thief, she would at least act the part. She spent the morning shopping for black cotton gloves, material to make a mask, and also some lengths of stiff wire and a pair of pliers, from which she could shape a set of skeleton keys.

She dined alone, then went up to her room to change, wearing a raincoat over her clothes. She slipped down her corridor and out through the fire escape, to where Hal was waiting in the car in a nearby side street.

'He and his daughter left just before seven,' Hal said as he set off for Ullmann's house. 'He was in a dinner jacket, so it looks like my information was correct.'

'Good.'

'I'll be parked in the next street. Any trouble, and I'll be straight there. But it'll be fine.'

'Right.'

They made their way to the Belgrano district. For once, Hal was driving within the speed limit. Perhaps it was knowing about the skeleton keys – hard to explain away if they were stopped and searched. But it was still far sooner than she'd expected that they were turning into a side street and coasting to a halt. With the lights and the engine switched off, it was very dark and still.

'Clemency?' he touched her briefly on the cheek. 'I'm sorry for biting your head off last night. You deserve to be taken a bit more seriously. I'll talk to Pryce-Jones tomorrow.'

She nodded. Focused on the job at hand, all that seemed remote and unimportant. She sipped out of the car, shed her coat and a few moments later was in the shadow of the back wall of the *Villa Rausch*. She pulled herself up and over, dropped to the soft ground on the far side.

There was no sound, no challenge, no dog barking. She ran to the back wall of the house. Again, all was silent. No footsteps, no whistling, no sign that any of the servants had stayed behind on what was supposed to be their night off. Then, far off, came the hoot of a train.

At the kitchen door, she drew out the skeleton keys. The lock was in good condition, properly oiled, and in a few moments the door was open.

Still she waited, listening, sensing the house, familiar and alien. There were the dark masses of shelves and cupboards, and gleams from the rows of hanging pans, ladles, knives. Carbolic soap overlaying the scent of stock simmering on the range. Flagstones cold through her thin shoes.

Not even a bolt on the back door? Did they want it to be easy for her? But if it were a trap, she had no choice but to spring it.

She walked through to the hall, conscious of moving further away from her route of escape, from Hal and the car and safety. She made no sound, feet placed carefully, a hand resting against the wall to guide her. The floor was polished wood, and there was beeswax mixed with the scent of flowers. A slight creak as the wooden frame of the house settled down for the night.

Then she was at Werner's study.

It was a little like Pryce-Jones' study, like Da
Silva's in Bern, like her own father's study that she'd
been forbidden to enter as a child, and which was still
foreign territory. All had the same sense of a single,
powerful personality, and of a maleness, where she
would always be an intruder.

She went to the painting by the fireplace and lifted
it carefully from the wall, revealing the safe. She spun
the dial and the safe door slid smoothly open. It was
larger inside than she had expected; several shelves of
bundles of papers. She looked through them. Diaries,
contracts, cheque book stubs, files of correspondence.
She began to drop them into her rucksack, but already
it felt anti-climactic. There was nothing bound in
leather, nothing remotely like the description of the
Covenant. Still, there might be something here that
would lead to it.

Then a blinding light stabbing out of the dark, and a
sharp voice telling her to raise her hands. As she did
so, the room lights were switched on. She recognised
the man by the door, a flashlight in one hand, a pistol
in the other, from the photo Peter had shown her.
Reinhard Werner. Beside him was the butler Jorge,
who held a shotgun, and a younger man, dark-haired
and as excited as Jorge was calm.

'Get down on the floor,' Werner said. 'Luiz, see if
she is hiding anything. A knife, perhaps.'

There was no choice. She lay flat on her stomach.
The man came over to check for a hidden weapon.
She flinched when his hands skimmed over her back,
her arms, down her legs.

'Nothing,' he said.

He stood up and Werner handed the shotgun back to him. He gestured for Clemency to stand. Then she saw another figure by the door. Petra.

Clemency's probing about her father's past must have been too clumsy, and Petra had gone running to him with the tale, and between them realised that Clemency had something like this in mind.

Petra came forward and pulled her mask away. She didn't react when she saw Clemency's face. This was only to prove what she already knew.

'You thought I would betray my father? He is a good man. A patriot. I am only sorry you were too stupid to understand.'

She turned and walked away. Not that there was anything Clemency could say. This was Petra's nature: clear, black and white. If Clemency was against her father, then she must be defeated and must suffer the consequences.

What would those be? They had Clemency by both arms. Even if she could have shaken them off, she wouldn't have had a chance of escape. That would have to be Hal's job.

They crossed the hall and came to the front door. Petra was holding it open. Her father paused for a moment.

'I don't think you need to come, my dear.'

They bundled her into a car and set off into the night. The way no-one had questioned her, demanded to know what she wanted and who she worked for, scared her. If they stopped to interrogate her, it would at least give Hal some time. But what if they just drove out into the countryside, somewhere quiet, where a shot in the night wouldn't be heard. That was the Nazi way. A bullet in the back of the head, then thrown into a ditch. Only now it wasn't a chilling story told by a survivor or a nameless victim in a grainy photograph. It was her.

Her palms were sweating. She was hot and chilled, and on the edge of shivering. Not knowing was gnawing at her resolve. Questions bubbled up in her. But they died in her throat because she feared the answer.

Hal. Hal would save her. He would be following. He'd have the training to deal with these cheap gangsters. She just had to stay alert. Luckily they hadn't tied her up. Over-confident.

They were near the river. Empty wharves, darkened warehouses, bleak expanses of concrete. A crane stark against the night sky. The river, she thought. A body would be carried away by the tide. Nothing to link it back to here. To them.

Anyone following them out here would be so easy to spot. Hal would have to keep back. Would he move quickly enough once the danger was clear?

They came to a set of chain-link gates. Jorge unlocked them and they drove in, to park in front of a long, low building, built of breeze blocks and with a corrugated steel roof.

There were no windows. That frightened her more than anything.

'Go and find Emilio,' Werner said to Jorge. 'Tell him to make himself scarce for a couple of hours.'

Emilio would be the night watchman. Whatever they had planned for her, they didn't want any witnesses.

Luiz opened one of the wide doors and she was hustled inside.

16

When the fluorescent strip-lights flickered on, the effect was blinding. Everything was white or steel: the white tiles on the floor and the walls; the steel of the roof and the steel of the pens and conveyor belts. There were odd pieces of machinery hanging from tracks bolted to the ceiling and served by thick black cables. When she looked closely, Clemency realised they were electric saws.

They marched down one of the aisles to the far corner of the abattoir, where there were more pens, and another high set of doors, and hosepipes ranged along one wall. There were drains in the tiled at regular intervals. This was where the animals would be brought in and hosed down before being stunned and killed.

'Kneel down.'

They stood around her, quite relaxed. Werner had put his gun away, but Jorge was behind her and would have the shotgun, and Luiz held a vicious-looking knife in his hand, the blade wide and curved and over a foot long, like a rapier-sharp machete.

'Now you tell us all of what you know.'

She stayed silent. After a moment, Werner nodded to Luiz, who stepped forward, took Clemency's arm and yanked it high up her back. She screamed, tried to rise up to ease the pain, only for his hand to push hard on the back of her head. As the pain ebbed, she opened her eyes. All she could see were the tiles, and Werner's boots. They were beautifully made, hand stitched, and quite pointed in the toe.

'What were you looking for?' he asked.

'Nothing.'

The pain came again, and she could feel the muscles in her shoulder tearing. She clenched her teeth.

'Shall I break it?' Luiz asked.

'No,' Werner said. 'Nothing must show.'

Instead, he nodded towards something behind Clemency's back. There was the sound of a cupboard being unlocked, and then Luiz was back, with a short baton, like a piece of thin steel pipe with a wooden handle. He was also licking his lips.

'Shall I strip her?'

'Oh no. The clothes will mean there are no marks.'

Luiz stepped forward. She raised her arm to ward off the blow; but instead of hitting her, he merely touched her raised arm with the end of the baton.

She was thrown onto her back, gasping with pain. Her arm was completely numb. Then Jorge stepped forward. He held another of the batons. She squirmed out of the way and pushed herself to her feet. But as she stepped back, Luiz was behind her. With a chuckle, he touched the prod against her bottom. Her back arched and her feet slid away from her and she was lying on the floor again, her legs twitching.

There was a moment's respite; then a voice.

'Who sent you? What did they want?'

She shook her head, crouched in a ball as Luiz tried to touch his prod against her groin. Instead it hit her thigh and she was flung against the wall, catching her head.

She lay in a world of pain, telling herself this wouldn't last forever. Hal would be there soon. He would have followed her. At this very moment, he would be readying himself. She hoped with every fibre of her body that whatever he did to them would be a hundred times worse even than this pain.

'Who sent you? What were your orders?'

'Go to hell,' she whispered.

Suddenly she was pinned to the wall by a deluge of water. Jorge was directing one of the powerful hosepipes on her, no more interested than if he were watering the garden at the *Villa Rausch*. She turned her head away so she could breathe, and then crouched, head bent, in the torrent.

Then it was over. The abattoir was suddenly very quiet. She could hear Ullmann's feet as he came to crouch at her side.

'Miss Black. Let us be reasonable. I have no wish to cause you pain. But I must have answers to my questions.'

'No.'

'These devices are for cattle. Cattle that are perhaps twenty times your weight. You cannot be expected to put up with this, can you? So why do you not tell me what I wish to know? Then you can go home.'

Only then did Clemency realise that she was not going home; not ever. Werner could not risk letting her speak of what she had found at the house, or what she had suffered afterwards. If she told them what she knew, they would kill her. If she did not, they would do the same – or torture her so much that she died on them anyway.

'I do not have all night,' Werner said.

'I was looking for money. Jewels. I'm just a thief.'

'Oh, you must do better than that,' he replied. He stood and stepped back, and his two men came forward. She tried to move away, but she was trapped. Three, four, five times she was caught by the prods until she could take no more and lay weeping and retching. For a moment, darkness closed in on her – a blessed respite.

She saw Hal, or was it Peter, striding into the room, a gun in his hand, shooting her tormentors one by one. Peter had her in his arms, and was carrying her out of this hateful place, and she could smile up at him so that his look of concern changed to relief, and he leaned down and kissed her. And then...

Then she was back in the real world.

The two men stood over her.

It was like a bullfight. They had danced around her, tormenting her, wearing her down; and now they were coming in for the kill.

Where was Hal? She'd lost track of time. But he couldn't be much longer.

If he were, it would be too late.

She opened her eyes. Werner was looking at his watch.

'You could end this now, you know. Just tell me what I need to know. Why make it difficult on yourself?'

His voice was so persuasive. She looked away. There was one chance. She remembered what she had been taught by Peter's wartime comrade Lucinda, about enduring interrogation. Tell them a version of the truth. Enough to throw them off the scent. Enough to stop the pain, if only for a while. She just needed an excuse.

'Who sent you?'

He was angry now. His fingers had locked around

her face, forcing him to look at her.

'No-one. It was my idea.'

He pushed her aside in disgust. Luiz was watching her avidly, the knife in his hand.

'Please,' she said. 'I don't know anything.'

Jorge put the prod to her neck. The pain was so intense she blacked out.

But the water brought her round. She slipped on the tiled floor, trying to sit up. It was easier to lie down and stare at the lights above.

'Are you waiting to be rescued?' Werner's question was laced with irony. 'Please put that thought from your mind. Your so-called fiancé? He has deceived you. You know that he has a woman? Maybe he is there now? In her arms.'

'That's not true,' she whispered.

'Where do you think he goes every night? The girls in the Boca, they are most appreciative of him. He pays well for their services, you see. For that, they are prepared to put up with his… unusual tastes. You know of those?'

Lies, of course. But it was the opening she had wanted.

'It can't be true,' she whispered.

'An unfortunate weakness of his. In Misiones, every night a different girl. So easy for us to find out his plans. Did you really think he cared for you?'

'He promised…'

'Yes, they always promise, don't they? But there it is. I expect he promised to keep watch. To keep you safe. But unfortunately, not. So…'

'I don't believe you,' she said: but less certain now.

'Believe me or not, as you wish. My patience is not inexhaustible. I had hoped we would not need to mark you. Then we could let you go. But perhaps it is time for Luiz. You should see him working with the knife here during the day. An artist. He can turn a carcass into nothing but cuts of meat in less than five minutes. Of course, the animals are stunned. They don't feel it. You, on the other hand…'

She turned to look at the knife.

'No! Please! I'll tell you everything.'

Luiz stopped his advance. If his disappointment were an act, it was a good one.

'I'm glad you've seen sense,' Werner said. 'Now, what do you know? Who are you?'

'I'm a policewoman. From Scotland Yard. Hal Linklater is my boss. He's trying to find a man called Schmidt. A Nazi. Because of the murder of some RAF men during the war. He thought you'd have something to help us find him. An address-book. He said you were the leader of something called ODESSA.'

'What else?'

'Nothing. That was it. They didn't tell me anything else. They said I didn't need to know. But I've worked undercover in one of the jewellery gangs in London. I know about safes. They thought that would be useful.'

He stared at her in puzzlement.

'A policewoman? From Scotland Yard? Jewel gangs? This is from the pages of Edgar Wallace.'

She had no idea what he meant. Then he began to laugh.

'To think I am followed by your famous Scotland Yard. And I am supposed to be Schmidt? And the head of ODESSA?'

Werner nodded to his two men and then walked off a little way. Still chuckling, he took out a cigar and lit it. Meanwhile they were putting the hoses away, locking up the cattle prods. Soon there would be no trace that they had ever been there.

'What about her?' Jorge asked. 'Do we kill her?'

Werner blew cigar smoke up the ceiling.

'What do you think?' he asked casually.

'It's safer. If she is from the police, she could cause trouble. She knows who we are.'

'True. But there will be awkward questions. Petra will be involved. No, I think we throw her back. After all, she has no powers here. I caught her breaking into my house. How was I to know who she was? No, I don't think the police here will care very much about what she says. After all, she knows nothing.'

She wanted to believe him. But as they dragged her to the car – she wasn't resisting, but could hardly walk – she thought of the alternative: that this was to make her believe she would live, until they took her to somewhere secluded and killed her.

There were two cars outside now. Clemency was pushed into the back of the one that had brought her there, while a chauffeur opened the door of the other and waited respectfully while Werner settled himself inside. He didn't look at Clemency, and soon he was driving off.

Jorge had taken a white linen butcher's coat that was hanging by the entrance to wrap around Clemency, but still she shivered in the night air. Luiz sat at her side, the knife loose in his hand. Lucinda had taught her the rudiments of hand-to-hand combat, but she could no more have tackled him that she could have wrestled with a lion. Every one of her muscles was in screaming torment, every nerve was burning. They put a hood over her head but she didn't resist. All she wanted was oblivion.

The car was moving through the city streets, quietly, not attracting any attention. It would be easy to follow it, but no-one was following. Was it true, what Werner had said about Hal? She found she didn't care. All she wanted was to crawl into a hole and forget him, the mission, everything. She would go home and never again think she could live in this world of betrayal and cruelty. She would forget her job, even forget Peter.

The car stopped. They pushed her out and she stumbled and fell onto a grass verge. The blade of a knife cold against her skin, and then the rope that had bound her hands was gone. The car drove off. Her clumsy fingers worked away at the ties of the hood. She pulled it off and breathed in the cool night air, the fragrance of frangipane and jacaranda.

She let time flow past. Then there was a flicker in the shadows. A cat walking along one of the high walls that guarded the villas on the street. It stopped and contemplated her with yellow eyes. Then it twitched its tail and stalked away.

She followed its path and then saw the familiar flag hanging limp. So they had dropped her outside the Embassy. A nice touch. She half-rolled over and pulled herself to her feet, made her way across the road and found the bell by the side of the gate.

In the end a bulky figure came out of a side door.

'Who is it? What do you want?'

She couldn't speak. It was the ex-sergeant-major, Harrison, and his solid, no-nonsense voice was everything she wanted. She would be safe now.

'Are you Mr Linklater's young lady?' he asked, already unlocking the gate and helping her through. 'Come into the gatehouse. He's been tearing the town up looking for you. I expect he'll call in again soon. But looks like what you need most is a cup of tea.'

17

A different kind of interrogation. Hal and Pryce-Jones sat opposite her while she sipped her tea and shivered under a blanket. Instead of bleak tiles, they were in one of the Embassy's formal rooms, furnished with impersonal good taste, a combined effort of the wife of the previous Ambassador and the Ministry of Works. They didn't show any concern for her having gone missing, or returning in a state of such distress. All they wanted to know was what Werner had wanted to know, and what she had told him.

'You are sure he was waiting for you?' Pryce-Jones repeated.

'Yes. It was a trap.'

'It was definitely you that he expected?'

She thought of Petra, coming up to her so confidently and pulling off the mask.

'Yes.'

'And they knew Hal was involved? You're sure on that point?'

She repeated Werner's warning that the two of them must leave the country within forty-eight hours.

'Did he say what he'd do if you stayed on here?'

'No, but as they took me out, they said something about Braun. Wasn't he the man we met in Brazil?'

'He's the head of their counter-intelligence bureau,' Hal said. 'If he's onto us, that's a problem.'

He and Pryce-Jones began to discuss the advantages of talking to their contacts in S.I.D.E. or the Federal police, while Clemency wondered if she might just die of pneumonia, sitting on the sofa in her sodden clothes.

When Harrison had said that Hal was tearing up the town looking for her, she could have cried, because it showed he cared. When he returned to the Embassy a few minutes later, all she'd wanted was for him to take her in his arms, and comfort her, and tell her that she was safe now, and that everything was going to be all right. Instead, he'd seemed angry with her, and Pryce-Jones had done little more than stare at her as if she were a half-drowned street urchin. All they wanted to know was whether their cover had been blown or not.

At last she was released, and Hal drove her back to the hotel. She was still in her wet clothes and Clemency felt this further humiliation as they were let in, even though it was only the night porter, who must have seen much worse over the years. Hal began to be more human, asking if she wanted anything to eat or drink. All she wanted to know was why he had abandoned her. She'd asked him once already, back at the Embassy, but Pryce-Jones had interrupted to say they'd come back to that, and of course they hadn't.

They stopped by the lift.

'What happened to you?'

'I was arrested,' he said with a rueful grin. 'I suppose they knew I was there, so they called the cops. They pulled up behind, asked to see my driving licence, said I'd been reported for loitering there in a suspicious way, so they insisted on taking me down to the police station to check my identity. It took Catsmeat an hour or more to convince them to let me go.'

The lift reached her floor.

'I'll see you in the morning,' was all she said.

'Clemency.' He held the lift door with his hand. 'I'm sorry. If there'd been anything I could have done. But short of shooting the police...'

There was nothing she could think to say.

'Goodnight, Hal.'

The bathroom was lined with white tiles and for a moment Clemency was back in the abattoir. But she was too cold to let those horrors stop her from stripping off her clothes in disgust, crying and sniffing, wiping her nose on the back of her hand, and at last she was standing under the shower. She poured too much shampoo into her shaking hands and rubbed it into her hair, letting the cleansing suds roll down her.

With them went some of her self-disgust and shame, and she found buried within her a deep satisfaction that she'd not only survived, but fooled Werner and kept the secret of the mission safe. She'd babbled about Scotland Yard almost at random, but for some reason Werner had been convinced. He would regret that. She would make sure of that.

There were bruises all over her, and angry weals where the cattle prod had touched her, and every part of her ached, and when she stepped out and reached for the bath robe, there was hardly enough strength in her arm to lift it down from its hook. She sat on a stool to dry herself and began to let herself think. Werner hadn't had the Covenant. More than that, he would never have believed she was a policewoman if he'd known about it. So they could scratch Werner from their list, and turn to Zoll.

Somehow, the pain and the humiliation of her interrogation was already beginning to fade. When

Werner had told her she had forty-eight hours to flee
the country or face the consequences, it had been a
relief. Of course she couldn't stay after this, but to be
told to go meant it was no betrayal. But now, all she
could think of was how to strike back.

She had flung her sodden clothes into the corner
before stepping into the shower. Now she picked
them up and rinsed them in the sink, then laid them on
the radiator to dry, ready for the next time she needed
them. She wasn't going to let Werner break her
spirit. Nor was she to blame for being caught. She'd
followed the orders she'd been given. It was Hal and
Pryce-Jones who had let Werner read their intentions
and set the trap, and Hal who'd left her there.

Peter wouldn't have done that. He would have found
a way to keep her safe. Or he would have planned
more carefully, so that the Link wouldn't have known
they were coming, or left a trap for him, or for her.

It was for Peter that she would stay.

◊

She slept late and only woke when Hal knocked on
her door to summon her to another conference with
Pryce-Jones. She dressed and went along to Hal's
room, where there was lunch laid out and where
Pryce-Jones, fresh, shaved, immaculate as ever, was
dabbing at his lips with a napkin.

'Ah, Miss White. A good night's sleep, I trust?'

Typically, he asked about her well-being in a way
that encouraged her to say that all was fine. She had
in fact slept badly, in a world of pain, which even a
handful of aspirin had done little to subdue.

'We've had a short council of war, and we thought

you'd like to hear our conclusions. That is, assuming you're happy to carry on?' he added as an afterthought.

'Of course.'

'Good. Well, we've certainly stirred up the hornet's nest. The thing now is to move fast. Werner gave you forty-eight hours. We'll use that time to wrap up the loose ends here, but by the end of it I want you out of sight. Ideally, they'll think you've gone back to London. Then you can make your move on Dr Zoll.'

'You know where he is?' Clemency asked.

'We do.' Pryce-Jones didn't say where he was and Clemency knew better than to ask.

'I'll have bookings made on the next BOAC flight out in your names, in case the Link have a contact at the airport. Now I really must get back to the day job,' he said, rising to go. 'You wouldn't believe how much time this cloak and dagger stuff takes up.'

He was picking up his hat and coat when Clemency interrupted him.

'I'd like to have a gun.' She'd meant it to sound reasonable, but instead it had come out as truculent. Not that it would have made much difference, judging by Pryce-Jones' expression.

'I don't think that's a good idea at all,' he said with distaste. 'Guns only complicate things.'

She looked at Hal. It was who had first suggested it, but he gave her no support now.

'Don't worry,' he said, with some of his old arrogance. 'I won't let you out of my sight until we're done.'

Pryce-Jones was still looking at her strangely, as if about to say something else. Then he nodded and was gone. Hal lit a cigarette.

'Annie doesn't get her gun,' he said. 'Never mind. I mean what I said about looking after you. Anyway, you can just stay in the hotel today.'

He dropped into a seat and then sat up in surprise, before producing a slim briefcase from behind him.

'That's not like Catsmeat. Usually so reliable.'

'I'll take it down to him,' Clemency said.

She took the case and ran to the lift. It was instinctive, and she knew she'd only have a few moments to scan what was inside. Luckily it was unlocked, and as before there was only one folder that looked relevant. As soon as the lift doors had shut, she began flicking hastily through it, one eye on the old-fashioned arrow that indicated which floor they were on.

Her nose wrinkled in puzzlement. The file held transcripts of telegrams, bundles of them, all marked secret. They weren't in code – the international telegraph companies like Cable and Wireless and ITT wouldn't carry coded messages – but were sufficiently cryptic to baffle her. Several of them mentioned Paraná and San Fernando, and she guessed they were telegrams within the Link, that Pryce-Jones had somehow managed to intercept. There was, she knew, some offshoot of the Foreign Office that could do this, though she'd never seen the product before.

It explained how it was that Pryce-Jones constantly knew more than he would admit; but the intercepts revealed nothing about the mission, nothing to dispel the clouds of ignorance that still surrounded her. The lift was passing the first floor, so she began to shove the folder back into place.

Then she saw the name Navarra, and the address of her office in Recolta. She didn't stop to study it. There was no time. But she had the gist. Someone was being instructed to terminate the contract with her firm at the earliest opportunity.

Now the doors were opening, and there was Pryce-Jones returning for his briefcase. She held it out to him without a word, managing a broad smile but not trusting herself to speak. The cover of using commercial language, enough to avoid giving away their true meaning in a casual inspection; but she guessed what it meant. The Link knew that Cristina Navarra had something to tell the British and had decided that she should be killed before she had the chance to do so.

'That's most kind,' Pryce-Jones said with a cold smile. She let the doors close between them, and then pressed the button to go to the top floor. She needed time to think. They had said nothing about warning Cristina. Yet they told her so little about anything. Maybe it was already in hand. Should she call Cristina and arrange to meet her? If the Link were planning a trap, it could close on them both.

She returned to Hal's room. He was reading the paper, a second cup of coffee to one side, and his pistol to the other. She poured herself a cup, weighing what to say.

'I thought I'd tell Cristina Navarra that we're going back to England unexpectedly.'

'That's a good idea,' he said, his mind elsewhere. 'See if she's picked up something useful.'

'Should we talk about that on the phone?' she asked. 'Surely there's a chance that the Link will have someone listening in?'

'I suppose so. Can you use the woman who gave you those tango lessons? Maybe arrange to meet there?'

'Of course.' So much for her being safe in the hotel, under his protection. Meanwhile he was hunting around for his cuff-links, preparing to go out.

'When will you be back?' Even to herself, she sounded like an anxious wife. Or maybe a nagging one.

'I'm not sure. It might be late. Don't wait up,' he added with a smile.

As she left to return to her own room, he was strapping on his shoulder holster. But whoever that was supposed to protect, it wasn't Cristina Navarra.

18

The cloud that had hung overhead all day was now settling down on the city like a thick and soggy quilt. Clemency found the start of Calle Cerrito without any difficulty. This would lead her all the way to Lucia's flat; but there was something unreal about the way the street, thin and narrow, disappeared into the tunnel of mist. There were few people about, and those wrapped up in hats and scarves. She shivered; and it wasn't entirely the cold.

She fixed her gaze on a blurred green light far ahead, and as the street descended towards the river it drew slowly closer, finally resolving itself into the neon cross of a pharmacy sign. Then it went out abruptly, and the dark closed in a little more. She began to think about who might be lurking in the doorways, and wished the street was a little wider.

At last she saw the light spilling out of the café opposite the café and a moment later was knocking on the door. Then she saw a note pinned up in spidery handwriting that she guessed must be Lucia's, though it was unsigned. *No hay clases hoy:* no classes today.

She tried the door again, stepped back into the road to see if there were any light on in the upper rooms, but all was dark.

She walked on, not wanting to be too conspicuous and taking the chance to puzzle out what she would do next. It was an hour's walk to Cristina's office, and she might have left by then. But there were no taxis, and she had no idea which bus to take.

Then she came across a phone box and asked the operator to connect her. Cristina's secretary informed her that *Licencia* Navarra was in a meeting, so Clemency had to hope that her message would be passed on and that Cristina would wait. Putting the handset down again, she looked about her. The little square was deserted. She felt very exposed there under the light in the phone box. What if they had been watching Lucia's flat? She felt stupid for not thinking of the risk, of assuming she was simply paying a call on a friend.

Peering into the mist, she thought of all the films where someone knows too much and is silenced – and so often in a phone box. Of course, it never happened to the hero or the heroine – but then maybe she was just a bit part who could be removed from the scene in a few feet of celluloid, just long enough to clutch her heart and sink to the ground.

She set off, alert for any signs she was being followed, but knowing that she might suspect nothing until the moment when she was bundled into a car, or someone stuck a knife into her back. It was bad when the streets were empty, but worse when there were people about, wrapped up against the damp and shrouded by the trails of fog. All she could do was to hurry on and hope.

It was nearly dark when she came to the Recolta district. It was getting hard to read the street signs but eventually she recognised an Art Deco garage she'd passed before and worked out that the cemetery was at the far end of the street.

Then she realised she was being trailed. There was someone behind; and ahead, she'd seen a man in a long dark mackintosh and a trilby hat cross the road once more than he'd need to, and each time he crossed he could look back and see that she was in place, caught between the two of them.

She stopped to admire a display of fashions in a shop window and tried to use the plate glass as a mirror to see if anyone else had stopped, but it was hopeless. She tried to remember the little she'd been taught about shaking off a tail. Should she run for it? Take shelter in a shop and demand that the owner call the police?

But what if they followed her in, claimed they were policemen, and took her away?

She was near to panicking. She'd been a fool to think that the night in the abattoir hadn't scarred her. She couldn't bear the thought of falling into their hands again.

There was nothing to do but walk on. The street joined another, with a high blank wall in front of her. She stood, undecided. Left would take her to Cristina's office, but was that only sharing the danger? Or making it even more certain that they would act? Right would take her past the entrance to the cemetery and into the unknown. Perhaps, though, she could jump on a bus and so keep moving.

She saw the two of them moving in on her, one behind, the other now on the far side of the road, in case she tried to double back on herself. She looked unconcerned, kept walking, and then dashed sideways through the high portico and into the cemetery. They would see her, of course, and follow her; but she had more chance of dodging them in the maze of tombs and narrow alleys than she did on the open streets.

She ran flat out down the path and into the first alley, not caring for the outraged glances of an elderly couple coming the other way. There were heavy footsteps behind her. She ducked left, then right, hoping she was losing them, but knowing she was losing herself. In the fog, the parades of tombs and catacombs were blurred, nightmarish, and it was impossible to keep any sense of direction.

From far away a bell began to toll. She stopped, and the hairs on her neck lifted, it was so much like a prison when an inmate had escaped. She had to get a grip. It was only to tell visitors that the cemetery was about to close.

Would they stay? She couldn't risk trying to leave. She would have to find a way out over the walls. Or stay there all night if she had to.

There were no sounds of pursuit. But that only meant that they too had become stealthy. And they would be armed. She slipped off her shoes and walked slowly forward, straining to hear any sound. The fog parted reluctantly before her, and closed up close behind. She was as likely to blunder into them as she was to keep out of their way, and once spotted…

She picked a tomb with an Egyptian entrance in grey stone that led back to a chamber topped with a lofty dome, the entrance closed off with locked iron gates. Using this as a ladder, she climbed up and tried to pull herself over the lintel. There was a stone cross and she used this to lever herself, only to feel it shift.

Letting go, she dropped back to the ground. Had they heard her? She was almost in tears from the pain of the fall, but she half-ran, half-limped until she found another tomb that she might be able to climb.

There was a convenient tree to get her started, and the roof was more solidly built, and soon she was flopping over the parapet onto a bed of dry leaves that rustled alarmingly.

Then she lay still, gazing up into the fog, listening.

For a long time, nothing. Then two sets of footsteps.

'Anything?'

'No.'

'Shit.'

'I'll watch the gates. There's no other way out. You go and call the others. Bring torches. And Bruno. He might smell her out.'

The younger man made to go, then was called back in a hissed whisper.

'And something like a ladder. If the bitch has any sense, she'll be on top of one of these fucking tombs.'

Silence descended. The man, dissatisfied, perhaps sensing at some level that she was nearby, walked back and forth. Then, with a more determined stride, he set off into the fog; presumably to guard the gate.

She had to go. Now, before they came back. Whether Bruno was a man or a dog, he was the one they were counting on. That, and a ladder. Even if they said there was only one way out, she had to find another.

The lamps along the main paths had been switched off, but that made things easier. She walked in as much as a straight line as she could, taking her time, listening out, making sure she made no noise, until she came to the outside wall.

Her heart sank. It looked even higher here than it did from the outside. Thirty feet? More? How on earth was she going to get over it.

She followed the line of the wall. Most of the time it was hidden behind ranks of tombs. She hoped for a tree with convenient branches, but in the end she found it easier to climb from the top of one tomb to another until one, so grandiose that it filled the entire plot, let her step onto the very top of the wall. The far side, facing onto the street, was sheer, but she walked along, arms outstretched, for fifty yards until she came to a tree.

A few moments later, she was standing on the street. Everything around was quiet. She still had her shoes, her bag, even her map. Had a cab come by, she might have flagged it down and demanded to be taken back to the hotel, or better still, the Embassy. But she was only a street away from Cristina's office. Unbelievably, it was not even seven o'clock.

It was Cristina herself who answered the door, and took in Clemency's dishevelled state, and fetched her some kind of rough brandy from the room of one of her partners. Clemency spluttered back to life and began to pour out her tale.

Apart from swearing under her breath, Cristina gave no sign of surprise.

'You were right not to go into a shop. They may be agents of the police, who are also working for the *Wachhund*. They would pick you up for questioning and you would never be seen again.'

The matter of fact way that Cristina spoke left Clemency chilled.

'How did you find this warning?'

'I can't say,' Clemency replied. 'But it's not a rumour. It's deadly serious.'

Cristina nodded, as if she had been expecting this day, had known she could not lead a charmed life, pursuing the Link yet immune herself, for ever.

'Do not worry. I have everything planned. There are

people who will look after me. If necessary, I will go to Montevideo for a while. The *Wachhund* would not try anything there. But it is frustrating.' She was pacing about now. 'There is so much to do. You and Linklater have stirred them up. This is good. It flushes them out. It worries their friends, who do not like trouble.'

Then she remembered that Clemency was there.

'You must go back. I am so grateful for your warning, and putting yourself at risk in this way. If there is any way I can repay you, I will do so. But you must go. So must I. You have the training so you are not followed?'

'Yes.'

Something, whether it was the brandy or Cristina's strength or the thought that she had escaped the Link a second time, had restored her confidence.

Cristina went back to the window, looking out but not expecting to see anything. Then she stiffened, like a pointer.

'Malditos ninos!'

She was straight out of the door, and clattering down the stairs, not wqiting for the lift, Clemency not far behind. She found Cristina in the street, walking towards someone crouched down by her car. The door was open, and Clemency could understand why she had thought it was kids breaking in to it.

But she was wrong.

The man turned, startled. His tail of his coat caught under his foot as hc tried to stand, and he lost his balance. Something slipped from his hand.

Then the whole car exploded into flames.

'Mierda!' Cristina said quietly. The man staggered forward, bathed in fire, and then fell to his knees.

Another man ran up, tore off his coat and began to beat at the flames. Faces had appeared at several windows. The burned man was screaming and his colleague began to drag him away.

The flames had turned Cristina's skin to red and her eyes flashed; but she was as close to being scared as she might ever be, imagining herself sitting in the car, the door closed, turning the key and then—

She couldn't drag her eyes away from the remains of her car, but she found her voice.

'Your source was good.'

'We should get out of here,' Clemency said urgently, but the flames were hypnotic.

'The police will come,' Cristina replied. 'I must stay. But I ask you to go to Lucia. She must not answer the phone, and she must not open the door to anyone but me. I will come there when I am free.'

Clemency was about to protest when Cristina reached into her handbag and then pressed something heavy into Clemency's hands. A gun.

'Please,' Cristina said. 'You and I, we are professionals. Lucia is…'

But it wasn't Cristina's words that persuaded Clemency to go. It was the fear in her eyes.

19

The room was in darkness, except for the streetlights casting abstract shadows through the shutters. They waited, listening to the life of the district, the passing cars, the footsteps and voices in the street, even the mewl of a cat on a wall below, expecting to hear a creak from the stairs, or the splintering of the frame as one of the windows was forced open.

'More coffee?' Lucia whispered. Clemency nodded, and Lucia moved soundlessly across the wooden floor to the kitchen. Her face looked sickly in the blue glare from the gas ring, but her hand was steady as she spooned out the coffee.

Clemency's plan was simple. If they came for Lucia, tried to break down the door, she would fire at them twice, and then shoot through the shutters into the street outside. That would surely cause enough noise to scare off the attackers. If not, she would still have three bullets left.

Lucia had a thin-bladed knife she had fetched from the kitchen. But thinking of the men who had taken her to the abattoir – what they had done, and what they could have done – Clemency had no illusions about the outcome.

Lucia handed her a cup and sat on the sofa beside her.

'How long will she be with the police?' she asked once more.

'I don't know. I wouldn't expect her for hours.'

They fell silent. There was a tension in Lucia that wasn't all down to the threat of being kidnapped. Once she made as if to speak, then thought better of it. Clemency guessed that they were thinking the same thing: why had the Link struck now? Was it because of the ambush on the Paraná, or Clemency's attempt to break into Werner's safe? But then why go after Cristina, and not Hal? Was it that they suspected – as Clemency herself was beginning to do – that Cristina knew something vital that she hadn't shared with her or with Hal?

And Lucia hadn't just been a friend who provided Cristina with a place to meet Clemency. She was much more deeply involved. Clemency knew this because of her silence. If this had come out of the blue, she would have demanded an explanation, showered Clemency with questions, drawn her into speculation. She had been horrified and upset to hear about the bomb, but not surprised. And she had accepted without question that Clemency was there to protect her.

The church bells chimed once more. Lucia sighed, ran her fingers impatiently through her hair. Stillness and silence were out of character, and the enforced waiting was playing on her nerves like an ill-tuned violin. She stood up abruptly, went to the edge of the window and peered through the shutters, careful not to be seen.

Clemency went to stand at her side. The street was quiet. There was no car parked with watchers inside; no man standing on the corner with a hat pulled down over his eyes.

'Will you tell your friend Hal of this? And your Sir Pryce-Jones?'

'Of course,' Clemency replied. 'They'll want to know where I've been, for one thing. But anyway, the bomb will be in the papers tomorrow.'

There was a movement further down the street; a scrap of shadow moving purposefully. But then it resolved itself into the loping figure of a stray dog foraging amongst the bins. Lucia let her breath out in a hiss and went back to the sofa.

'Why did you ask about Hal?'

'I thought he might help to get us away,' Lucia replied. It made sense, but Clemency didn't believe her. More and more, she was convinced that Lucia was holding something back, yet wanted to confide. But though the silence stretched out again, all she did was lie back and contemplate the shadows on the ceiling.

After a while, Clemency felt her eyes becoming heavy. She yawned hugely.

'We must stay awake,' Lucia announced. 'You must tell me everything about you.'

It was a little like the way she had talked to keep Hal awake on the long drive to Misiones, except that, from time to time, Lucia would stiffen beside her, and they would wait, tensed, willing the footsteps to pass on, until Lucia, who knew the sounds of her own street so well, would relax and lie back and tell Clemency to carry on. Or she would tell her stories of her own childhood in a small town in Patagonia, where her father had been an engineer and her mother a schoolteacher. How she had dreamed of an escape to Buenos Aires, of turning the scratchy sounds of tango from the shortwave radio into her life.

In this unreal, intimate setting, when time was marked out only when a nearby church chimed the passing hours, Clemency found herself talking of Peter. Not by name; but to explain to Lucia why she was caught up in this world of espionage.

'I swore I would get him back. He must feel so alone. It's been six weeks. Of course, he's no idea I'm doing this – that I've taken his place.'

'He will know,' Lucia replied. 'Not that you are in Buenos Aires, with a gun in your hand; but he will know that you would never forget him. That you are doing everything for him. That you will always care for him. When you have been lovers, then—'

'We weren't. Not like that.'

'Then you are…?' Clemency could see Lucia's teeth smiling widely, see the amusement in her eyes. 'You love him with such passion that you come to other side of the world, you risk your life, you are ready to point a gun at a man and kill him, all this for this man – and yet you have done no more than kiss him? Oh, but I am sorry. I do not mean to make fun of you. It is just that you are so very English.'

'What do you mean?'

'They say it is we are the ones who love with such passion.'

'Well, don't you?' Clemency replied, nettled by this mockery. 'Isn't there a boyfriend you could call to come and help us out?'

'No. I have never loved a man like that.'

Lucia spoke with a strange edge to her voice.

'Oh,' Clemency said. Then she realised what Lucia meant. 'Oh.'

Now there was a very different tension in the air. Clemency's skin tingled with fear, but not of guns or spies. It was the fear that rose from the half-understood depths of her own desires. Like Hal, like Lucia, she was scared, and she wanted to be touched, held; loved.

You are shocked?' Lucia asked teasingly.

Clemency couldn't reply. Lucia had taken her hands in hers. Her legs were stretched out to both sides of Clemency's. It couldn't be more intimate. Yet it didn't feel wrong.

Lucia, it seemed, was content to wait to see what Clemency did next. She leaned back, resting her head on the arm of the sofa, and wriggled a little to make herself more comfortable.

'People think that to be a dancer of tango, you must be *lasciva*. You understand?' Lucia added, seeing that Clemency didn't. 'Too sexy. Dirty. But it is not so. You must know exactly how far to go. How far you want to go. How to tell your partner without words what you feel. What is pretend. You see?'

'We're just dancing?'

'Exactly. Is this easy for an English woman to understand? I do not know. I have no English friends.'

'We're a long way from England.'

'There are many English here in Argentina, but they are so cold, and so sure they are better than everyone else. I have Italian friends, and French, and German, and Armenian. But not English.'

'Maybe you haven't met the right ones.'

Lucia didn't seem to hear.

'Still they have a hold on us all. They are, perhaps, what we want to be. They are calm, and sensible, and they organise everything the way that suits them. They do not wave their arms around or swear at each other. They do not have scenes and cry. They do not put knives into each other for love. They are not corrupt or criminals. They lack so much. Yet they have something we cannot have.

'You were so cool, dancing with me. Like dancing

with a ghost. With a creature made of ice. I have never felt anything like it. I wanted to... And now you laugh at me. That is so English. I can see what you are thinking. You will take my words about fire and ice, and turn it into a joke and say that fire and ice makes steam or something silly like that.'

'It's true,' Clemency confessed.

'You wrap yourself round with ice, but this is my chance to be close to you for a little while. If you do not mind.'

For a moment, Clemency thought of her mother, of her friends, of Hal and Pryce-Jones. Of Peter.

'I don't mind.'

◊

It was nearly dawn when the call came. The clattering of the phone was like a thousand dropped pan-lids after the hours of silence, and Clemency jumped awake and found Lucia clutching her arm. But after three rings it stopped, and they relaxed, and sure enough it rang again to show it was Cristina. Lucia's face lit up with joy and relief as she heard Cristina's voice. Their conversation was too rapid for Clemency to follow properly, but the gist of it was that she would be there in a few minutes in a car with 'some friends'. Clemency guessed that Cristina, with her usual efficiency, had arranged for armed protection.

Now it was time to part, Lucia was touchingly concerned for Clemency's safety.

'You must leave Argentina,' she insisted. 'Go home while you can. What if the bomb in the car had been for you? This mission of yours – is it worth it?'

Clemency reassured her she would soon be gone.

She had been identified by the enemy, her usefulness was over, and she would certainly be called back to London.

When she was gone, all Clemency wanted was to find somewhere quiet to sit and think. But she could almost feel Hal's impatience and anger that she had not made contact. With a sigh, she picked up the phone and called the hotel.

◊

Hal picked her up from a nearby café an hour later. He was silent, preoccupied, but not, it seemed, through anger with her. It was as if he were turning over in his mind some complex plan, and her role, and Lucia's fate, were very minor parts.

'We've got your stuff from the hotel. There's a safe house – well, a flat – where we'll regroup and plan the next stage.'

'Can we do that? I thought if we'd been identified, we couldn't carry on.'

'It makes it more difficult,' Hal conceded. 'But we've got to see it through. Particularly as we know something no-one else does – not the Link, not the KGB. Only us. We know where Zoll is. The trick will be to get out of this city without being spotted. Then, we've got him.'

Somehow the prospect of bringing the mission to a successful end couldn't raise her spirits. She was too drained and found herself yawning.

'Busy night?' he asked with his usual mocking glance.

'So-so.'

'I'm touched by the idea of you standing guard over

Sabatini. I hope it wasn't too nerve-racking.'

There was something odd in his voice.

'What is it?' she asked. 'What is it I don't know this time?'

'Your friend...' He checked the mirror and then swung into a side road, enjoying letting the silence drag out.

'Well?' she asked.

'It's just there's something priceless about the situation. I'm sure you were very brave to take it on. But of course, you were in no actual danger.'

'How do you know?'

She could still see the flames billowing out of Cristina's car; and remember what it was like to be hunted through the graveyard.

'An educated guess. You see, why would the Link want to kill Sabatini, when she happens to be working for them?'

'What? She can't be!'

'Oh, Clemency.' His voice was laced with pity. 'The first rule of an intelligence officer is not to trust your instincts. She's been part of this from the start.'

'But she's Cristina's... she works for Cristina Navarra. Is she a Nazi too? And what about that bomb? Am I making that up too? I saw it.'

'Hey, whoa, don't blame me. As it happens, we think Navarra is what she says she is, and is working for various socialist and Jewish interests. But Lucia Sabatini is working for the Link. Why do you think Catsmeat was so interested in hearing that Cristina had introduced you to her?'

'Why didn't you tell me?'

'Innocence is the best mask of all. And you do it so well.'

'But she could have killed me. Or told the Link where I was and had me picked up.'

'They could have picked you up any time. After all, they had you in their hands, didn't they, and they threw you back. So there was never any real risk of that.'

'Have you told Cristina? Warned her?'

'That would reveal a source of information that I'm afraid we have to protect at all costs. I'm only telling you know because we're leaving Buenos Aires and you won't be in contact with either of them again.'

'But...'

Clemency looked out of the window at the passers-by making their way to work, waiting for buses, sitting in cafe, reading papers. Living ordinary lives, in which people were roughly what they said they were, and the ones you liked you could usually trust.

Between her and them was a gulf that was greater than a sheet of glass.

'Don't feel so bad,' Hal said, with a hint of compassion. 'I don't think its ideological. I expect she needs the money.'

'Does that make it better?'

Hal thought about this for a while.

'Well, it makes it different.'

20

For two days they stayed in the flat, seeing no-one, bored but with an undercurrent of fear, so that every time the elderly lift creaked into life, Clemency thought of the *Wachhund*.

Most of the time, she sat in the window, reading or more often looking down on the Avenida de 25 Maya, the scurrying cars and buses, the specks that were people. It gave an illusion of an ordinary life, rather than the reality of semi-imprisonment.

She was reading Sorokin's latest thriller, *Moscow Agent*, about a GRU colonel fighting Western mercenaries in a newly-independent African state. It had been translated from Russian into Spanish, and somewhere along the way the life had drained out of it, leaving the characters to perform like marionettes against an over-complicated plot.

Sorokin himself had delivered it the day after the dinner, taking the chance to inspect her hotel room and quiz her about her life in London, her family and friends. She'd assumed it was his writer's curiosity, but Hal was convinced he was snooping at Comrade Maliakov's request. Another thing for them to disagree about.

Like cell-mates, they got on each other's nerves. Hal was constantly fidgeting. He'd pick up the newspaper, then spend most of his time folding and unfolding it, reading an article for a few moments, rustling the pages, then throwing it aside. He'd whistle tunelessly between his teeth, pace up and down, glance impatiently out of the window.

The more he fretted about being unable to go out, the more she showed how patient she could be, calmly turning the pages. The more incessantly he smoked, the wider she opened the window.

It was a relief when it was time for her to prepare a meal, though it was almost all tinned food and she could hardly blame him when he pushed the mysterious meat and the canned vegetables round his plate disconsolately.

At last, Pryce-Jones returned with a busy, jolly woman in her sixties whom he introduced as Mrs Smith. She was English, though Clemency guessed she had lived in Argentina for many years because she spoke like a character in a light comedy of the 1920s.

'Are these the victims? I'll start with you, my dear.'

She took Clemency to the bathroom and began the process of transforming her into a chic young Spanish woman of the upper class: her hair dyed black, her eyebrows thickened and resculpted, and while Clemency sat back and let it happen, Mrs Smith let forth her life story. An affluent childhood, running away to go on the stage, her talent not matching her ambition, a second-rate theatre company touring Shakespeare and Noël Coward around the Empire, and then ending up in Buenos Aires, married and settled, but with a hand in all the amateur dramatics to remind her of her old life.

What she didn't need to say was that, when England called, she was happy to help out and would not breathe a word.

'There you are, then, dear.'

When Pryce-Jones had told her of her new identity, she had thought it ridiculous. His reasoning was that they risked being caught out in any disguise, because they had so little time to prepare their back stories and Argentina was such a melange of different nationalities that even pretending to be Latvian or Romanian could land them in trouble. It would be so easy for an emigré to pursue them with questions about the old country. Hal's Spanish was excellent and he was confident he could pull off the part of a Spanish minor aristocrat, who would be expected to be stand-offish. Clemency could keep in the background, looking suitably disdainful, and if she did speak, anyone who had doubts about her Castilian Spanish would simply think she was originally from another country before her marriage.

She stared at her new identity in the mirror, practicing looking haughty, raising her chin, even flaring her nostrils. It worked surprisingly well – perhaps it was the new arch to her eyebrows – and for the first time she thought she might be able to pull it off.

◊

They drove out through the southern suburbs, the grand avenues giving way to factories and warehouses. The houses seemed to shrink as they went, from apartment blocks to villas, then bungalows made of roughly-plastered breeze blocks, and then – right on the edge, where the flat of the pampas began – there were shanties of wooden packing cases and roofs of tarpaulin. After that, they picked up some speed, overtaking the empty trucks returning to collect more grain, meat and vegetables – above all, meat – to feed the maw of the city.

At last they reached the town of Brandsen, built up around the railway station. Everything was like the Wild West – the tracks separated from the road by a post with two crossed planks on it; the lonely station building, with no platforms, just an expanse of dust and gravel; a rusting water tower.

When the train arrived, it looked the part, for each carriage had an open platform at each end and the name of the railway company ran along the length of each one above the windows in gold paint, although instead of Baltimore and Ohio or Union Pacific it read *Ferrocarril General Roca*.

'Another bloody general,' Hal muttered as they climbed aboard. 'No wonder they can't keep out of politics.'

Though the train was quaint from the outside, it was at least as luxurious as the equivalent in Europe, with wooden panelling and crisp linen bedding and even a bottle of mineral water sitting in a little holder by the head of each bed. The conductor, short and friendly and sharp-eyed, took the pesos that Hal offered with dignity and assured them that they would have a most pleasant journey. Then they were left alone, as the train began to pick up speed.

'You'd better take the top bunk,' he said, lying on the bottom one with great satisfaction, his jacket falling open so she could see his gun holster. 'Not that I'm expecting any trouble. Catsmeat had it all well-organised, didn't he?'

She wasn't so sure. It was a relief to be away from Buenos Aires, and the safe house. But throughout the mission they had been outsmarted by the Link. They had found about her searches in the archives. Ullmann had slipped through their fingers. With his daughter's help, Werner had laid a trap for her. Had they really shaken them off this time?

The day wore on, and the train made its way across the flat landscape of fields and wide rivers, groves of trees and occasional farm buildings. They stopped in a succession of sleepy towns, where she joined Hal in climbing down from the train for a few minutes. It helped relieve her tension to walk up to the front and gaze along the tracks running straight towards the horizon. But there was something so frustrating about the hissing of the engine, the occasional clank as the steel of the frames and wheels contracted. All that power standing idle, when they should be off and on their way. The Link could be in a car, hurrying through the night to overtake them. They could even fly and be waiting at Bahía Blanca, ready to strike.

The train had felt like a means of escape. But as darkness fell, turning the windows to mirrors, reflecting Clemency's anxious, strained face, it became a prison. There was none of the urgency and exhilaration of the express trains of Europe, cutting through the night at a hundred miles an hour. So many stops, and at each one the Link could put one of their agents on board.

Then Hal was beside her, not touching her but very, very close.

'You're tensed up,' he said.

'It's not a surprise, is it?'

He didn't reply, but instead began to massage her shoulders, his strong fingers exploring and then starting to work away at the knotted muscles.

'You've been under a lot of pressure,' he said gently. 'You need to relax.'

She closed her eyes as he pressed his thumbs into the line of her spine, while pulling her shoulders back. Little waves of pain and pleasure ran down her arms. She rested her head against the cold glass of the window. Then he was guiding her to lie down front-first on the narrow bed.

'I'm so proud of you, Clemency. You've been through so much. The archive, the ambush, being taken by Werner...'

'Aa-aaah...'

He was using his weight to press more deeply into her back, and it was on the edge of hurting, but she didn't want him to stop.

'You're a very brave girl. You know that, don't you?' His fingers reached the base of her spine, still exploring. 'But you don't need to bottle it all up inside. You're not alone.'

'What do you mean?' she said, her words a little muffled by the pillow. He took his time replying, and his hands kept working at her muscles and tendons, drawing the tension out of her like a magician.

'I'm not one of those dinosaurs who think women don't have the same needs as anyone else.'

His voice was gentle, persuasive.

'Deep down, I know what you want. Probably more than you know yourself. Oh, I don't flatter myself. Any half-decent man would do. It's the nature of the job. The fear, day after day – it's looking for a release.'

It was half-true. She wanted to turn to him, between those strong arms, feel him holding her, kissing her, letting him make love to her as the train rattled along through the night, until at last she would sleep and wake and everything would be all right. She wanted this – no, craved it so strongly that it was like a drug.

Then she thought of Peter. He might have felt the same urges as Hal, but he wouldn't have thought to take what she had gone through in the last few days and use it to prise her open.

So while part of her wanted him, another wanted to slap him. As Pryce-Jones had said, he was in charge of the mission. He was her commanding officer. She just had to endure this.

'Hal…' Her hands took his, her smile was sweet and sad. 'Let's talk about this when the mission is over. It's just… you know…'

Meaningless words, but they did their job. He could convince himself that she felt something for him, and that was all that his ego really needed. He relaxed, nodded. They were back to normal. In a few moments, he was suggesting they go along for the second sitting in the dining car, and helping her on with her shrug, opening the door for her. Safely back in the strait-jacket of the modern Englishman.

Later, after dinner, she lay in her bunk, thinking again of Peter. In some ways, he and Hal were similar: the same turns of phrase or ways of thinking that came from boarding school and military service. There were moments – seeing his hands lying firmly on the steering wheel, or catching a hint of his aftershave, when she could have been mistaken for thinking Peter was at her side. But beneath the hard shell, Peter was a man who could be trusted. And Hal? At their first meeting, she'd seen a hint of cruelty in his eyes. Nothing since had proved her wrong, whether it was the way he'd laughed at the old ferryman, floundering in the riverside mud, frightened out of his wits; or how he'd left her to be taken away to the abattoir by the Link, rather than risk his cover.

The train rolled on into the night, the swaying and rocking becoming hypnotic. The dinner of steak and the heavy Argentinian wine had dulled her senses. Clemency began to doze, thinking of how falling for Peter had saved her from Hal. Otherwise, she might now be lying in his arms, making love to the awkward rhythm of the train. Peter and Hal became confused in her mind, so that it was Peter who had burst into her hotel room and pinned her back on the bed, Peter who had held her close as he showed her how to fire the machine gun; Peter who had danced the tango, shown her the steps, encouraged her to feel the passion of the music – except that it was Lucia who was holding her, leading her...

'There's still time for breakfast, if you hurry.'

Hal's words brought her back to consciousness. He'd pulled up the blind and daylight was flooding in. She rubbed her eyes.

'We're just coming into Bahía Blanca,' Hal said. 'We're here for a while. Changing engines, I think. I might go for a stroll and pick up a paper.'

He was already dressed and shaved, and as soon as the train slowed to a halt he was on the platform and sauntering towards a bookstall. She took in the florid Edwardian plasterwork, the high roof glazed like one of the hot-houses at Kew Gardens, then pulled down the blind and began to wash and dress.

All around were the sounds of passengers coming and going, bags being passed onto and off the train, occasional shouts of greeting from the platform outside. The people had been much more warmly dressed than in Buenos Aires, and despite the train's steam heating Clemency was grateful for her jacket as she made her way to find some breakfast. The light cotton frocks she had bought for Misiones would not be much use in the southern autumn, let alone once they were in the Andes. She had traced the route out of Argentina on Hal's map and was imagining the Paso Puyehue, high up in the mountains, where they would cross over to Chile. At least she still had the riding boots.

She entered the restaurant car. There were a few travellers there, lingering over their morning paper and coffees. She wondered if the waiter could be persuaded to find her some pastries.

Then the man at the table beside her looked up.

'Miss Black! What a pleasant surprise. Please, do join me.'

It was Anton Sorokin.

21

For a moment, Clemency thought of pretending she didn't know him, that he had mistaken her for someone else. But under his sharp, amused stare she had no choice but to do as he said and take a seat opposite her.

'Such a coincidence,' he said. 'And Mr Linklater, he travels with you?'

'Yes.'

'I almost did not recognise you,' Sorokin went on, enjoying himself. 'You have changed your hair?'

The waiter came up and she ordered coffee distractedly.

'Your Spanish is so good,' Sorokin continued relentlessly. 'No trace of an English accent.'

'Thank you.'

'And what is this?' He turned over her book. 'Aha, Borges. He is, of course, a reactionary. I have never read him.'

'It's all I have. I've finished *Moscow Agent*.'

'Truly?' Sorokin beamed in delight. 'I trust you enjoyed it?'

'I liked the way the hero is happily married, and keeps trying to get messages back to his children. But why did you have to kill off Natasha?'

'It pained me to do so, but it was necessary for the story. Did she not die beautifully?'

She was saved from having to reply by the arrival

of her coffee.

'Are you travelling to Bariloche?' she asked.

'Unfortunately, no. I go only as far as Carmen de Patagones, where I am to lecture to the local union of teachers. I hope it will be another success. Buenos Aires was a triumph. But tiring,' he added with a smirk, and lowered his voice. 'Even in Argentina, there are communists. They yearn to know more about the worker's republic. Some are young, passionate for justice. The girls, they have the most passion of all. For justice, and for other things. What could I do?'

'What indeed.'

'And you and Mr Linklater, you go on to Bariloche, then?' He snapped his fingers. 'Ah! But of course, you are in disguise! You travel as man and wife. Am I not right? How romantic.'

He knew perfectly well who they were. Maliakov would have guessed that Hal was with SIS and shared this with Sorokin. It didn't necessarily mean that either of them knew why Hal and she were in Argentina, or the purpose of their visit to Bariloche. But she had a horrible suspicion that Sorokin knew more, perhaps knew everything. He liked feeling superior to others – and this meeting was giving him enormous pleasure.

'You have seen the newspapers?' Sorokin asked her. 'It seems we have all chosen a good moment to leave Buenos Aires.'

He held the folded paper out to her. She took in the headlines, and the grainy picture of the blackened remains of Cristina's car.

'The police are saying it is the work of a criminal gang. Of course, we know it to be the work of Fascist elements, do we not?'

'Do we?'

'This lawyer was involved in bringing some German exiles to court last year. It seems to me obvious that reactionary forces are wishing to make an example of her. Do you not agree?'

'I don't know much about Argentinian politics,' she said, wishing she could hide behind her coffee cup, away from Sorokin's amused gaze.

'For some reason I thought you might know this... this lawyer, Navarra. No?'

'I've only been here a few days.'

'Yes, I forget. Yet you are to make your life here, while I am about to leave. Is Señor Linklater to join us?'

In his whimsical way, Sorokin suddenly seemed to tire of teasing her. Instead, he gave her the benefit of his views on the contents of his newspaper: colonialism, wars, American imperialism, British decline. She began to relax a little. Even if Maliakov had shared his suspicions with Sorokin, they were hardly likely to reveal this to the Link.

Her conviction that Sorokin was merely enjoying himself grew when he lit a cigarette and blew a jet of smoke into the air above them.

'When you appear in my next novel,' he began, 'you will be the young assistant to the British super-spy. He will be in Argentina to arrange the overthrow of the elected government. This will be to prevent British investments from being taken into the ownership of the people. Assets such as the very railway on which we are travelling, and which was paid for by British capital and by the exploitation of the workers. But perhaps you will have some qualms of conscience.'

'Will I?'

'Yes. Now I think of it, who better to be my model

for that super-spy than your fiancé? He will be making common cause with the Nazi elements who infest this country. But you cannot bear this. Perhaps your father died at the hands of the Nazis during the War?' He grimaced, his face so much like a clown she had to smile. 'No matter, there will be a motive. You warn the hero, and the coup is prevented.'

'A happy ending.'

'Yes. Unfortunately not for you. You will need to be killed by the super-spy.'

'That's a shame,' she said dryly. He shrugged.

'There is a… a necessary shape to these things. We Russians, you understand, lost so many in the Great Patriotic War. Husbands, sons, even daughters. We know that you cannot have victory without sacrifices. But I will make sure you do not suffer. A bullet to the heart. And then – ah, and here is Comrade Linklater.'

He stood politely as Hal joined them, and then made his excuses: a speech to write for his event that evening. She was relieved to see him go, but he left behind the knowledge that if Maliakov could trace them so easily, then so could the Link.

Hal must have had the same thought. She noticed that, even as he was laughing at the idea of a little fat man like Sorokin being any concern of theirs, his hand had strayed to the gun in its holster beneath his jacket.

And from then on, at each stop, Hal would climb down to the platform and light a cigarette, making a point of stretching his legs and looking around at the local scene, while scrutinising anyone joining the train. To Clemency, it was a futile ritual. Agents of the Link would look just like any of the other passengers. They would find it easy to blend in because this was

now their country, and they could play themselves –
the harassed businessman, the priest standing aloof,
even the couple in heavy fur coats waiting impatiently
for the porter to catch up with them.

Even their destination had an air of unreality,
this town of Bariloche that everyone said was like
a lakeside resort in Switzerland, yet could only be
reached across this dry, flat desert of thorn and dust.
Her nagging fear was that they wouldn't try anything
on the train, because they didn't need to; because
she and Hal were so helpfully moving themselves
towards the trap.

At Carmen de Patagones, Sorokin came to their
cabin to say goodbye, saying – surely with irony –
that he hoped they would one day come and be his
guests in Moscow.

'When you have settled into your new estate,' he
said to Clemency, 'you must send me your address
via the Embassy. Comrade Maliakov will forward it.
Then I will send you my next novel. I am sure you
will enjoy it. I hope too that you will enjoy Bariloche.
It is an ideal place for lovers. You will not ever want
to leave.'

They watched him climb down onto the platform
where he was met by two tall, well-dressed men who
had the self-importance of senior academics, and
Clemency tried to convince herself that he had told
the truth and that he really was on the train as part of
his tour.

For something to do, she walked the length of the
train, seeing if anyone looked at her twice. But there
was no-one who seemed out of place, no furtive
glance. Everyone was caught up in their own world
of tedium, chatting or playing cards, reading or just

staring at the grey world outside.

Eventually she came to the platform at the end of the final coach. She leaned on the rail and watched the tracks slowly unwind through the empty plains. With each mile, there had been less to see. Fewer buildings, roads, fields. Now there was hardly a sign that the land had been settled at all. When Lucia has spoken about the vastness of Patagonia, Clemency hadn't really understood. Now she could feel what it meant, could see why it would breed a kind of loneliness, a sense of insignificance, like spending your life staring up into the infinity of the sky.

Over dinner, watching the sun set over the flat empty land, Hal explained that they wouldn't return to BA but instead go on from Bariloche over the Andes and into Chile. Faced with his absolute assurance that he could deal with Dr Zoll, something inside her snapped.

'Do you have a plan for Bariloche?'

'See the sights,' Hal replied, missing the acid in her tone. 'Take a boat out. Go hiking. We're tourists, remember. We have to establish our cover. Then we can call on Dr Zoll.'

More and more, she mistrusted the inevitability of how Ullmann and Werner had been false leads, and Zoll their real quarry, as if the mission were a fairy tale or a three-act tragedy. But when she tried to express her conviction that they were heading to disaster he quickly waved that aside.

'It's natural you're feeling jumpy. Remember, you're not used to all this. First there was Misiones. Then BA was serious stuff towards the end. You don't forget something like that overnight.'

It was true she hadn't shaken off the fear, and

sometimes her anxiety shaded into paranoia. She'd even thought that she'd seen Lucia boarding the train at the last stop, until she'd realised it was a nurse who happened to resemble her. But that wasn't what was draining away her confidence. It seemed foolhardy to be heading to Bariloche, Dr Zoll's home turf, with no support, no contact, even, except for Pryce Jones.

The worst was the long corridors in the sleeping cars. Anyone could be waiting behind the row of blank doors. She'd have no time to escape, even to cry out. And this time, the Link wouldn't worry about leaving a mark on her. It would be a wire around her neck, and then her body sent tumbling from the train, into the night.

She could take the risk, but only if she knew what the reason was.

'Hal, I've decided something. I can't do this if I don't know why we're doing it.'

'You don't need to know.'

'I do. I'm sorry, but I just can't keep my courage up. All afternoon I've been more and more convinced this is a trap. The Link know about us. They're probably laughing at us.'

'They don't know we're here.'

'I don't want to let you down. But if I have to, I'd rather do it now than if we do walk into trouble. So I'm going to get off the train at the next station. I'll make my own way back to London from there. I'm sorry.'

'Scared?'

If he were trying to rile her, it didn't work.

'Yes. I'm scared. But that isn't the reason. It's because I can't work in the dark. I know more than you think, but it's still not enough.'

'What do you know?'

'About the Covenant.'

He went very still. Only his eyes moved, glancing at the empty table behind them. Then he leaned forward.

'What do you know,' he repeated, quietly, slowly.

'Only that it's the reason we came here. It wasn't because of what these three people have done. It was to find out which of them had it, and get it back. Isn't that right?'

For a moment she thought he was going to strike her. His eyes seemed to have glazed over, and there was a rigidity about his face, his whole body, as if ready to spring.

Then he smiled.

'You're full of surprises, Clemency.'

He drained his glass.

'Let's go back to my cabin. It's time I told you what this mission is really all about.'

22

They lay side by side on the bottom bunk, her head in the crook of his arm, his lips close to her ear. He'd insisted on this, so that even if their cabin were bugged, there was little chance of his whispered words being picked up over the rumble and rattle of the train. She didn't object. The sexual tension of the night before had gone. She was calm, filled with confidence. It was not knowing the truth about the mission that had been gnawing away at her, sapping her resolve. Now, she was to be led into the heart of it.

'Everything that Pryce-Jones and I have told you so far is true,' Hal began. 'But not the whole truth. That was partly for your safety, but also because if you'd known what this was really all about, and they'd squeezed it out of you, it would have been a catastrophe. That's no reflection on you or your courage. It's just a matter of fact. Need to know and all that.

'But I can't finish this off without your help, and so now you really do need to know. Zoll was in the Luftwaffe and he did carry out those experiments. What I didn't mention was that these were with radioactive materials. You see, Dr Zoll was one of the top scientists working on the atom bomb for Hitler. When that project was wound down, in around 1943, the Luftwaffe didn't drop it completely. Perhaps developing an actual atom bomb would cost too much and take too long, they thought. But what about a dirty bomb, that wouldn't create the same explosion but would still spread contamination over hundreds of square miles? That was what Dr Zoll was working on, with his human experiments. He was researching radiation sickness.'

'That's so horrible.' Despite the heat of Hal's body, so close to her, she shivered.

'If that was all that Dr Zoll had done, then he'd just be another Mengele. Ancient history. But Zoll is a greater danger now than he ever was. You see, the reason Perón and his people tracked him down and got him out to Argentina in '47 was that they wanted to build an atom bomb of their own. That's what Zoll is working on.'

'Here? In Argentina?'

'A placed called Huemul. It started with Perón thinking about atomic reactors to make energy for all the new factories he was building. But the army wanted it because the atom bomb is the ultimate weapon. There's also the rivalry with Brazil. That's the only other country in South America which has the resources to even contemplate an atomic weapons programme. The Army started to wonder what would happen if Brazil had the bomb and Argentina didn't. Although on the surface, this is a civil project reporting to the ministry of technology, the Army is pulling the strings.

'If they build a bomb, then think what that means for Brazil. They'll throw everything at getting one of their own. Perhaps Chile too. But our real fear is whether the Argentinians might try and recoup some of the money they've spent on all this by selling the know-how to others. They're in secret talks with the

Egyptians about building a reactor, and that could be cover for weapons. There's even some suggestion they'll do a deal with the Israelis. With the Soviets backing Egypt and the Americans behind the Israelis, this could start a third world war.'

He fell silent, letting it sink in.

'Is this what the Covenant is about?'

'In a way,' he replied. 'Over the years, the Argentines have poured millions of dollars into Huemul. But never enough for Zoll. He's had rows, threatened to resign, and it seems to have made him a little paranoid. The Argentines keep him on a tight leash. A small salary, restrictions on his movements. They don't trust him, and he doesn't trust them. So he decided he needed an insurance policy, in the shape of a very large amount of money in a Swiss bank account.

'All the top Nazi scientists who came here after the war signed a Covenant to work for the restoration of the Third Reich in Germany. It has all their names. He offered to sell it to us through Sabatini. We didn't know that it was him until we'd eliminated the other two possible sources of the approach. Now that we've done that, it all falls into place.'

'So he was the one using Lucia as a go-between?'

'Yes, but she won't have any idea who he is. Or where. That's why he thinks he's safe, a thousand miles from BA.'

'How do we make contact with him?'

'Baroloche lies on a huge lake. In the middle of the lake is the island of Huemul. It's like Windscale or Harwell, with reactors and laboratories, exclusion zones and searchlights and armed guards and the rest of it. Beyond top secret. This is where Zoll works. We can't get at him there. So it has to be at his home.'

'Where's that?'

'About ten miles along the shore. You see, Zoll is still key to the whole thing. Remove him, and the project will be put back five years.'

'So this was never really about the Covenant?'

'No. Once we knew Zoll was one of the three people who might have it, we realised it was a chance to get at him. Usually, we couldn't approach within ten miles of him. He's too important to the Argentinian military, and too well-protected. But because he wants to trade the Covenant for a suitcase full of cash, he's going to let us walk right up to his front door.'

'And then we... remove him.'

She knew what it meant. Kill.

'There's no other way,' Hal said. 'We can't drag him back to Britain. It has to be something more permanent.'

She fell silent.

'But now you see why it matters so much?'

'Yes.'

'And why we didn't tell you this? It was so important that he had no idea we weren't after the Covenant, but Zoll himself. If that had got back to him – through Sabatini, say – it would have been the end of it.'

'I see now.'

'Good girl. Look, it's getting late. We've got a big day tomorrow.'

She got ready for bed, settled down in her bunk, her head still swimming from everything Hal had told her. He began to clean his teeth.

'You know, it's a bit of a relief to be able to tell you all this at last. No more secrets. I meant what I said about how well you've done on the mission.'

He spat into the basin.

'By the way, how did you find out about the Covenant?'

'I just caught sight of the word on some papers Pryce-Jones had on hs desk.'

'And you thought it might convince me you knew more? You are a tricksy one, aren't you?'

He turned out the light and heaved himself into the upper bunk.

'Anyway, no more spying or prying, eh? You're on the inside now.'

'Of course, Hal. And thank you for trusting me. It was not knowing why we were here that was so hard.'

She lay in the silence and the darkness. She'd long known that the mission wasn't about bringing Nazi war criminals to justice. That wasn't how people like Hal and Pryce-Jones and their superiors in London worked. The Covenant had seemed like the answer. But now Hal had told her that even the Covenant was only a means to draw Zoll into the open.

Zoll was the real prize. A man who was central to a conspiracy that could tip the precarious balance of the Cold War into nuclear confrontation. Kill him, and millions of lives might be saved. Against that background, the mission finally made sense.

Except that Clemency knew that everything that Hal had just told her was a pack of lies.

◊

They'd finished breakfast and were lingering in silence over a second pot of coffee. Clemency was gazing at the distant white line on the horizon, the snow-covered ramparts of the Andes. She was lost deep in her own thoughts. They would soon arrive in Bariloche, find their hotel and spend the afternoon settling in and checking for any signs they were being watched, and letting the watchers relax if they were. A pleasant meal, a walk along the lake, an early night – and the next day they would kill Dr Zoll.

She had to admit that Hal's plan was a good one. Zoll knew that the British were coming to buy the Covenant. He'd be suspicious that they planned to double-cross him. The chalet was isolated, and anyone approaching would immediately be suspect, whether they came by car over the single-track road or by boat from Bariloche. To try and reach him on foot, through the forests, might succeed, but it would make it almost impossible to escape again once the deed was done.

'A girl, on her own, out on the lake in a boat that's broken down,' Hal had said. 'He won't be alarmed.'

That was the essence of Hal's plan. They'd each hire one of the motorboats kept for tourists in Bariloche, head separately out onto the lake, then rendezvous on the nearest island to Zoll's chalet. Hal would fix the engine of her boat so it would run rough and splutter whenever she wanted it to, and then she could approach the chalet, seeking help. She'd cut the engine at a convenient moment and then row the boat into shore, being careful not to be too competent. Zoll would come to help, and she would produce a pistol and hold him until Hal arrived.

Then Hal would kill Zoll. It wouldn't be in a struggle or in self-defence. It was to be an execution, and she would be the only witness.

Hal muttered something and left the table abruptly, but she hardly noticed. The lack of sleep, the motion of the train, the thought of Zoll's death, all conspired to make her feel queasy. She poured herself more coffee, but it was mainly dregs. Typically, Hal had helped himself to almost all the first pot and most of the second.

She jumped as she was touched on the shoulder.

'Señora Ruiz? Your husband is feeling unwell. Could you come with me?'

She rose without thinking and followed the conductor along the length of the dining car, struggling to keep her balance and admiring the way he seemed to anticipate every movement, so he didn't need to hold the seat backs. Like a sailor, she thought to herself inconsequentially. With the regular swaying of the carriages, she felt a little seasick herself.

'Do not be alarmed, Señora. There is a doctor in cabin nine and he is already tending to your husband.'

Something was calling out to Clemency from the back of her mind, but she was too tired to concentrate. It was easier to follow the conductor through the next coach to the far vestibule, where a small crowd had gathered. There was the doctor, tall, authoritative, straightening his jacket a little as he pronounced the result of his examination, that it was probably some kind of food poisoning, or possibly a severe bout of gastric flu.

It was all so unreal. A few minutes ago Hal had been complaining of a headache. Now he was lying unconscious in the corridor.

The nurse of the evening before appeared, prim and starched in her immaculate white uniform. She had the doctor's bag and she passed him an ampoule and syringe. She kneeled down and began to roll up Hal's sleeve while the doctor drew a clear fluid into the syringe with a grunt of satisfaction.

Clemency's eyes were drawn back to the nurse,

because she was Lucia.

The next thing Clemency knew the conductor was gently lowering her to the floor, and calling to the doctor. She couldn't speak, or resist, and had to watch as the doctor looked down on her, felt her pulse, raised one eyelid. He made a satisfied sound, but nothing to the look of triumph in his eyes. And Lucia had a cool cloth and was dabbing it tenderly on Clemency's forehead, her eyes full of mischief, and saying over and over that she had nothing to fear, while the thin needle slid into Clemency's vein.

23

Clemency was dreaming. She was on a hospital trolley.
There were masked faces looking down at her. A doctor
and a nurse, swaying side to side because they were
in an ambulance. The nurse was Lucia, smoothing the
hair from Clemency's forehead, her hand beautifully
cool.

Then the doors opened. They must be at the hospital
now because of the scent of pine. Lucia was filling a
syringe from a glass vial, and then had her arm, and
the sting of the needle was real, and Clemency almost
woke up. But Lucia's eyes were so kind, so loving, that
she knew she was safe.

She slept.

◊

Clemency awoke on a bed in a bright room with
wooden walls and the smell of pine and fresh paint.
She could see a patch of sky, the tops of a stand of trees,
and beyond the almost shocking white of a range of
mountain peaks. She remembered being ill on the train,
and something about an ambulance, except that it was
all still mixed up with the dream. There was a bandage
across her lower face, but she was not in any pain. In
fact, she felt well, and safe, and quite content to lie
there. She'd never have thought a hospital could be so

lovely and so restful. There was no noise, no shouting in the corridor, no sour smell of sickness or overcooked food. The only odd thing was that she couldn't move.

She tried to wriggle free, but it was like being under sheets that were tucked in too far, and she had a picture of a no-nonsense nurse pulling the blankets drum-tight. Her arms were wrapped around her, over her stomach. She craned her head and saw she was wearing some kind of white canvas jacket, and her legs were secured to the bed with a series of straps.

Perhaps she'd had a fever, been raving, and they'd done this to keep her safe. It amused her. She'd heard about straitjackets, but never thought she'd end up wearing one.

She lay back, head on the pillow, suddenly very tired. Peter. Where was Peter? Was he all right?

She looked to her side. There wasn't a bell to call the nurse, and in any case she couldn't have reached it. She called out, but the bandage across her face muffled her words. Just like a gag.

It didn't seem to matter. That was the strangest thing of all. She was trussed up, tied to a bed in a strange place that looked less and less like a hospital, and yet she was so calm. It was easier just to watch the wind in the trees and the sky over the mountains.

◊

When the door opened Clemency jerked awake. It was nearly dark outside and the nurse came and put on the bedside light. Clemency assumed she was dreaming again because Lucia was wearing a nurse's uniform, right from the cap on her head to what looked like white tennis shoes on her feet. She even had one of the little upside-down watches pinned to her front.

'How are you feeling?' she asked.

'Mmph.'

'Oh yes, you must not speak. I should not be here at all. But are you thirsty?'

'Mmph hhmph,' Clemency replied, before realising that nodding would be more effective. But Lucia seemed to understand well enough. She poured a glass of water and then unwound the bandage across Clemency's mouth.

'You must not make a noise,' she said sternly, but she cradled Clemency's head as she drank.

'What's going on. Where am I? What are you doing here?' Still Clemency was curious rather than angry, or afraid.

'So many questions,' Lucia replied, squeezing her arm reassuringly. 'Do not worry about anything. You have to stay here for a few more hours, that is all.'

'But why?'

'Dr Zoll insists. He says it is better if you wait here until the payment had been made. Then you are free to go.'

'So we've been kidnapped?'

'Of course not.' Lucia was almost shocked. 'The Covenant is waiting for you downstairs. But Dr Zoll is a very cautious man. He did not want to put your friend Hal into temptation to take the dossier and perhaps forget to pay.'

'Where is Hal?'

'In the next room. He has sent instructions for the delivery of the money. Now we wait the arrival.'

The drink of water had cleared Clemency's mind and she was beginning to feel scared. If Hal had agreed to this, it should be all right. He would hardly hand over the money if he thought they would be killed anyway. Yet she could not be more helpless. Meanwhile Lucia was fussing around the room, adjusting a vase of flowers, straightening a chair, playing the part of a hospital nurse and enjoying it hugely.

'Lucia, please, you've got to let us go. You can't really be working for those people. You know who they are, don't you?'

'Of course,' she replied, glancing instinctively at the door. 'But you must trust me. You are quite safe, and all will be well.'

'But if—'

'I insist,' she interrupted sternly. 'The patient must rest.'

Appealing to her better nature hadn't worked; perhaps there was another way.

'There's one other thing. I've got this awful itch on my back. Could you scratch it for me?'

Lucia sat beside her on the bed. She slid her cool hand inside the straightjacket, and her nails began to dig deliciously at Clemency's skin.

'Dr Zoll would be very angry with me,' she said.

'Why?'

'Perhaps he does not trust me with you.'

'Perhaps he's right.'

Lucia's expression changed: amused, with a hint of disappointment.

'Tell me,' she said. 'What is your true name?'

'Clemency.'

'*Clemencia?* It means the same? Forgiveness? Yes, that is right for you. Yet you are thinking how you can kill me and escape. It is true,' she said, laughing as she stood up again. 'You are a spy and you have been trained to kill with your hands, no? So I will leave you tied up until you remember that I am your friend and that soon you will be free.'

'How soon?'

'If you want to talk, tell me of your life in England. Do you know the Queen? Has she given you a medal for being the best of her spies? Oh! The Beatles! Have you met them?'

'Seriously, what is this all about? Why were we taken off the train?'

But Lucia heard her name called from below. She went to the door.

'Yes?'

'Bring her down,' a man's voice called out.

Lucia untied her legs and helped her to sit up. Then she led Clemency down the stairs and into the main room. Large windows ran along the far wall, giving onto the lake, looking cold and uninviting now that the sun was behind the mountains.

It was the doctor from the train. He had the confidence and authority of a surgeon, and it was no great deduction to conclude that this, at last, was Dr Zoll.

She felt no aura of evil, no great threat, beyond the fact that she and Hal had fallen into his hands. He was in that sense quite ordinary, though he would have been handsome in his time and was still, in his sixties, distinguished.

It should have been a dramatic moment. This was the man they had come to kill, who had so many deaths on his conscience, and was working on a bomb that could destroy millions more. But he didn't welcome her with sinister charm, or bark threats, or even suggest he was that interested in her presence. He merely nodded to her and then turned to Lucia.

'We are losing time. The schedule says we must have

begun the next stage by now.'

'Shall I bring the Englishman down?'

'No,' he said impatiently. 'One is enough to take care of. I must go and make the signal. It will take no more than twenty minutes.'

Without waiting for her to reply, he handed her the gun and pulled on his gloves.

'If she moves, kill her.'

'Of course.'

Lucia stood with feet apart, with a cruel smile of anticipation, as if was waiting for the excuse to do just that. Zoll nodded in satisfaction.

'Good. They tell me she is as cunning as a fox, this one. If you are not careful, she will kill you for sure.'

He left the room. They waited in silence, listening to him opening and then closing the front door. His heavy tread could just be heard along the path.

Then silence.

'I think it will take him longer than that,' Lucia said conversationally. 'He is not a man of action, is he?'

'I suppose not,' Clemency said. She was puzzled by Lucia's tone, but she had to agree. It was hard to imagine Dr Zoll actually killing anyone. He was more like an actor playing the part of a ruthless man.

'But it will be time enough,' Lucia added.

'For what?'

'Escape, of course.' She was amused by Clemency's bewilderment. 'You think I really work for the Nazis? But the story of how clever we are must wait. Go and release your friend. I will search the house. We must be gone before the doctor returns.'

Lucia began pulling open the drawers of the sideboard, pushing aside the rows of glasses and piles of plates. Bewildered, Clemency sensed that behind the confident, amused manner, Lucia was a little scared. So she hurried up the stairs and found Hal tied up in one of the rooms, awake, his eyes burning with anger above the wide bandage that covered his mouth.

She knelt down and began to pull at the knots, but Hal had struggled against them for so long that they were too tight for her to have any chance of undoing. She ran back down to the kitchen, slipping on the wooden stairs in her stockinged feet, so she had to grab the rail to save herself. Lucia looked up and laughed.

'You think we want a broken leg?'

'I need a knife.'

She found one in the kitchen and in less than a minute Hal was shaking off the bindings and trying to bring some life back to his arms and legs.

'How long have we got?'

'Zoll said he'd be twenty minutes. That was five minutes ago.'

He nodded.

'Who were you talking to?'

'Lucia. The nurse,' she added, remembering Hal had never met her. 'She was on our side all long.'

'Funny way of showing it,' he said, crossing to the window.

'Lucia's searching for papers. But we can go any time.'

'Oh, I don't think we want to leave Dr Zoll without saying goodbye, do we?' Hal said. 'That would be rude.'

He walked stiff-legged to the top of the stairs and eased himself down, grimacing as the blood worked its way back into his muscles. Lucia was kneeling by a cupboard.

'What have you found?' Hal called out.

'Do you not wish to thank me for saving your life?'

'Save the smart lines for later,' he said, then turned to Clemency. 'Have you got a cigarette?'

'You know I don't smoke.'

'A cigarette?' Lucia said, producing a case from the front pocket of her uniform. 'Allow me.'

He took one and let her operate her lighter for him. His fingers were still stiff. But once he had drawn in the first draft, and breathed it out with a deep-felt sigh, Clemency began to relax. Hal was a going concern once more.

'I'll take the gun,' he said.

Lucia handed it over willingly, then turned to Clemency. 'I have never fired such a thing. When Dr Zoll said I might need to shoot you, it was hard not to laugh. Did you see?'

'I thought you played being a ruthless killer surprisingly well.'

'I was good, was I?' she replied. 'For a while, I was the most evil woman who had ever lived.'

Hal glanced at his watch.

'Right. You sit here,' he said to Clemency, pointing to the sofa. 'And you stand here, he added, pushing Lucia into position. 'I don't want him to be suspicious. Right?'

Footsteps approached. A few moments later, Clemency caught a slight movement from the corner of her eye. A face at the window. Zoll surveying the scene. Then he unlatched the door and eased himself inside.

Clemency had slipped her hands behind her back and tucked her feet out of sight beneath the chair, as if she had been tied to it. Zoll was reassured, but still puzzled. He frowned at the doors of the cupboards hanging open.

'What is all this?'

'I was looking for some more rope,' Lucia replied, without turning.

'It is time to bring the Englishman down.'

'No need.'

Hal stepped out of the shadows, the gun trained on Zoll, who could do nothing but gape, and then turn in astonishment to Lucia.

'What is this?' he said. 'What is happening?'

'Simple,' Hal said. 'You turned the tables on us. We turned them back again.'

He was enjoying this more than he ought to; but he gave Zoll no opening as he advanced into the room.

'Get his gun,' Hal said to Clemency. She crossed the room, keeping out of the line of fire, and reached into Zoll's pocket, where the gun lay cold and heavy. She stepped quickly away, and handed it to Hal. He nodded his approval, not taking his eyes from Zoll.

'Where's the Covenant?'

'Here. But in my safe. I will—'

In two steps, Hal had crossed the room, and he smashed his fist into Zoll's stomach. As the man doubled over, he hit him again, then twice more, until he fell and lay crumpled and moaning.

'Don't you dare tell me what you will or won't do. You will do exactly what I say. It is marginally more convenient for me to let you live, but if you cross me again, I swear to God I'll snuff you out like a candle.'

The gun held lightly in his hand, Hal crouched down beside him.

'I thought this was all tolerably obvious, but let me now explain. You are going to give me the Covenant. We are still going to pay you for it, because I don't want any trouble before I leave the country. You'll be tied up here, and when we're well across the border, we'll let someone know where you are. You see?'

Zoll nodded wearily, and began to work his way onto his knees.

'It's so much easier once you accept reality,' Hal said conversationally. 'You see, I could just kill you and break into the safe myself. Or rather, Miss Black here could use her considerable skills in that department to open it up. How long would you say? Twenty minutes?'

'If that,' she replied in the same casual way, taking her cue from Hal. She was still mystified by Hal's attitude. Didn't he want to eliminate Zoll? Or at least take him away for interrogation? But she knew better than to question his lead.

Resignedly, Zoll had crossed to the safe and was kneeling down, his hand resting on the combination dial, awaiting the inevitable.

'Run upstairs and get some ropes, will you, Caroline? The ones he used on us.'

Clemency hurried upstairs to the room where she had been kept. The ropes lay coiled where Lucia had dropped them. As she turned to go, she couldn't help but glance out of the window, where the lake lay like tarnished silver in the twilight. Far away, just beyond the headland opposite, a launch was approaching.

Then came a shot from below. Two more in quick succession. She ran to the top of the stairs and called out.

'Hal?'

'It's OK.'

His voice sounded natural, if a little strained. Then she caught a whiff of gunsmoke. She held the bannister and went down, taking every step carefully.

In the lounge, Zoll lay on the ground, not moving.

Lucia was crouched beside him. And Hal stood a little apart, a gun in one hand, and a maroon folder in the other.

He glanced up at her.

'He tried to jump me.'

She knew it was a lie. Hal's tone. Lucia's sickened expression. Hearing about Zoll, she had wanted him to pay for his crimes. But not like this.

Now she could hear the sound of the boat out on the lake, drawing nearer. From where she was standing, she couldn't see the path down to the jetty, but soon the engine cut out, and in the silence she heard footsteps approaching.

Then there was a rat-a-tat-tat on the door. Such a comforting sound, like the knock of a postman back in England.

'Come in,' Hal called out.

The door opened. There, looking both ludicrously out of place, but also very much at home, was Jacob Price-Jones.

'Well, here we are again.'

24

They were a team again, just like on her first day in Buenos Aires. Hal the professional. Clemency the useful underling. Pryce-Jones, fastidious, detached, yet in control.

'How do we leave things, Hal?'

'A robbery. Zoll is forced to open the safe. Then he's shot. We leave it for someone to come and find him and call the police. That might not be for days, out here.'

'And her?' Pryce-Jones asked, nodding to Lucia, now sitting on the sofa, her arms wrapped around herself.

'It turns out she wasn't working for the Nazis at all. She was the one who set us free.'

'Was it?' Pryce-Jones turned to her. 'Well, Miss Sabatini, it seems we owe you a debt of thanks.' Pryce-Jones gave a little bow, and it was hard to know if he were mocking her or not. 'I take it you don't mind seeing one of the Fascists receiving his just desserts?'

Clemency was willing her to play along. Surely she must see the danger?

'No,' Lucia said, her voice expressionless. Then she glanced past Pryce-Jones and saw Clemency. There was an appeal in her look, as if she could not cope with any more.

'It must have been a shock,' Clemency said. 'But I'm sure Lucia will cooperate.'

'Ah, yes, you know her as well, don't you?' Hal

turned to Clemency. 'Good to know we're all on the same side. I must say that when Miss Sabatini first approached me about the Covenant, she gave a rather good impression of being a Fascist herself. But maybe that just goes to show what a talented agent she is.'

'I helped Cristina by making the acquaintance of some of the Nazis.' Her explanation was aimed at Clemency, as if she felt guilty for having kept the truth from her. 'It was through them that I was approached by Zoll to be a go-between. He told me to contact Señor Pryce-Jones at the British Embassy. It was no trouble. I wanted these papers to reach the British. I did not mind if they paid. The British, they have no shortage of money.'

She managed a faint smile, but her eyes strayed back to the dead man on the floor.

'I couldn't have had a more charming agent to deal with,' Pryce-Jones said gallantly. 'Now, to business. Miss Black, could you and Miss Sabatini tidy up? All the bannisters and door handles and so on will need to be cleaned. No fingerprints. Check there is nothing left in the rooms. Bring the luggage down to the jetty. We must make sure there are no traces that we were ever here.'

Obediently, Clemency led Lucia through to the kitchen. As soon as the door was shut, Lucia seized her arm.

'What are we to do?' she hissed. 'How do we escape?'

'It's over,' Clemency replied. 'Zoll is dead.'

Lucia's eyes held anger as well as fear.

'There was no fight. Zoll was no danger. He did not try to run or to take the gun. It was an execution.'

Clemency had guessed as much, though she'd tried to bury the thought.

'The man was evil, Lucia. He killed many people. Tortured them. We don't owe him anything.'

Now Lucia had her by both shoulders, her words tumbling out so fast Clemency struggled to understand.

'He sent you away. He didn't want any witnesses. You see? You might suspect. But you cannot say you saw him kill Zoll. But I? He let me watch. Why? Because I do not matter. Because I am to be killed.'

'That's not going to happen.'

'You will stop them? How? You have a gun? You have friends who are to come and save us?'

'No.'

Lucia broke away in frustration, and stood by the sink, her head down.

'They won't harm you. I promise.'

'Should I run?' Lucia said, more to herself than to Clemency. 'But where? I do not know where I am.'

'Trust me.'

Lucia looked up. The passion was gone. She smiled a little sadly.

'He will kill you too, I think. You can see in his eyes that he is a cruel man. And the tall one? He will not care. For him, it will be business. For the English, that matters more than anything.'

'But...'

'Come. They must not suspect.'

Lucia found the broom cupboard, and handed Clemency a duster and a can of polish.

'I will begin upstairs.' But before she left, she opened a drawer, picked out a short, sharp knife and dropped it into the pocket of her tunic.

Back in the living room, Pryce-Jones was sitting at the desk, going through the drawers as if he had all the time in the world. Hal was searching the rest of the room more violently, upending chairs and cushions and spilling books onto the floor.

Clemency began dusting.

'Is there anywhere upstairs we need to search?' Pryce-Jones asked her.

'Something could be hidden,' she replied. 'But the bedrooms are very plain. I don't think this place is used much.'

'No,' Hal agreed. 'There are no papers, no photographs, nothing personal. Even the books are random. Nothing on science, no periodicals.'

'Maybe this isn't his place. Or maybe he rents it out.'

Talking like this, a team once again, it was impossible to think she was in any danger. But she dared not ask them what was to come next, and what was to happen to Lucia.

'I think we're done here,' Pryce-Jones said, easing himself to his feet. Lucia came down the stairs, carrying the luggage that had been taken with them from the train.

'Just put it there,' Pryce-Jones said casually, pointing to the doorway. It was the same voice he would have used to talk to his maids in the house in Recolta. Unimportant. Interchangeable. Replaceable.

Lucia nodded and went back upstairs for the rest. Pryce-Jones crossed to the coffee table and picked up the maroon folder.

'We should destroy that now,' Hal said.

Pryce-Jones made a point of considering.

'You mean in case we're stopped? I think we can afford that risk.'

'It's what we agreed.' Hal's voice was quiet but emphatic. 'I'm going to burn it, here and now.'

'Don't be a fool. This is vital for us.'

'Why? So you can blackmail these people?'

'Of course not,' Pryce-Jones snapped. 'There are fifty or more names. This gives us a ready-made anti-Communist network right in the heart of the Government. If Wilson and his useful idiots win the election, we'll need them. You must see that.'

'Look at the list.'

Puzzled, Pryce-Jones opened the document again and turned the pages. He went very still as he cast his eye down the page.

'I see.'

'Yes. My father. That's why it goes no further.'

'We wouldn't do anything against him. I give you my word.'

'I can't take that risk. After all, you'll have to pass the Covenant to others, won't you? I might choose to trust you, but that doesn't bind anyone else, does it?'

'Then we're at an impasse.'

The seconds passed as the two men faced each other and Clemency, forgotten, looked on. At last, she understood why Hal had been so careless about the fate of the Covenant, even to burning out Werner's *estancia*. He'd always wanted to destroy it. No wonder he'd been driven to pursue it with such venom, with his family name at risk. His own father a traitor, conspiring with the Nazis and planning the death of Churchill and the King. If that came out, he'd never live it down. No more evenings at his club, no more regimental reunions or society weddings. Ostracised. Shamed. Enough to turn him slightly mad.

'All right.' Pryce-Jones handed him the dossier. 'Unity in our movement is more important than anything. We'll do it your way.'

Hal took the file with a curt nod. He took out his

lighter and knelt down by the fireplace. Pryce-Jones came and stood over him. And before Clemency knew what was happening, and long before she could cry out, Pryce-Jones had produced a gun and aimed it at the back of Hal's head. As Hal flicked the lighter into life, Pryce-Jones fired.

Hal gave a strange animal groan. He toppled slowly into the fireplace, then rolled onto his side. His eyes were staring into space. Puzzled, perhaps.

Then, nothing.

For a long moment, they both looked at the body. In his long black coat and gloves, Pryce-Jones could have been a mourner at a funeral, communing with the open grave. He even seemed to be saying something under his breath. A prayer, perhaps.

Meanwhile, Hal's body had stopped twitching.

'I had no choice,' Pryce-Jones said, still looking down. 'He disobeyed his commanding officer in the field.'

Clemency could say nothing. The horror of what she had witnessed was already giving way to fear. Like Lucia, there was no way Pryce-Jones could let her live.

'Wait over there,' he said, nodding to the sofa. Then he went to the foot of the stairs and called up to Lucia to fetch some towels and a sheet from one of the beds. A few moments later, she came into the room, slowly and fearfully, clutching a bundle of linen tight across her chest, as if it would protect her from a bullet.

'Mr Linklater is dead,' Pryce-Jones said. 'We can't leave him here. Wrap the towels around his head, then roll him into the sheet. Miss Black will help.'

It was a horrible job. Hal was still warm, and even his face had not yet taken on the waxen mask of death. Touching him to roll him onto the sheet reminded her of how they had laid close together in their cabin on the train, and he had spun her yet another web of lies.

Pryce-Jones stood over them while they did as he directed, wrapping the sheet around him, tying it close, and fetching some heavy fire irons to weigh it down. It was clear enough that Hal's last resting place would be in the lake outside. Clemency wondered if she and Lucia would be joining him.

Between them, they carried the luggage out to the launch, and then came back for the body. Then they were put to a final cleaning up, scrubbing the small pool of blood by the fireplace, all that Hal had lost in the few seconds before he died.

Then they were done.

Clemency and Lucia carried him out to the launch, with Pryce-Jones behind them. Then a return journey for the luggage. They were to be killed, that was clear. But not here.

He made them go down into the cabin, so even the chance of jumping into the water and swimming for it was gone. He switched the engine on, cast off the rope and took the helm, and soon the boat was moving away from the shore. After a few minutes, they were far out into the lake. Pryce-Jones switched the engine off.

It was suddenly very quiet, and very lonely. There were no lights along the shore, only the massed ranks of fir trees crowding down to the water's edge, and the high mountains behind, black against the indigo sky.

25

Hal's body was laid out at the stern. Pryce-Jones could tip it into the lake without taking his eyes off the two women crouched in the cabin. An oily splash, and he was gone. The luggage followed, and then they were setting off again.

It was all so logical. Pryce-Jones could shoot them and dump them into the lake, but there was nothing to make them sink. Their bodies might be found, and it would not look like a burglary gone wrong. There might be blood in the boat, too, and that had probably been hired in his own name. So Pryce-Jones had to find some other way to dispose of them.

She only wished she could think as clearly as him, but her mind kept jumping to the horror of what was to come, the unfairness, the loss.

'What is the Covenant?' she called out to Pryce-Jones. The question came at random, but anything would be better than the despair that threatened to envelop her.

'Hal never told you?'

'He told me nothing.'

He didn't reply, and didn't look at her, keeping his eyes on their course. Perhaps he wanted to avoid any human contact, anything that would make the duty of killing her any more difficult.

'Why did he have to die? Isn't it all ancient history?'

'Of course not,' he snapped. 'You think the Communists have gone away? 1945 was only a ceasefire. The people who signed the Covenant weren't wrong. They were only ahead of their time. They could see that Communism was the danger to England, not Fascism. That was why they signed.'

'What did it say?'

'It was a pledge.' He was looking at her now. 'Fifty of England's leading men, committing to a government that would preserve England and the Empire. Even if that meant replacing Churchill and the King.'

'Replace them? With who?'

'You don't understand,' he replied. 'None of your generation do. You don't appreciate what a gamble Churchill took in 1940. Hitler offered him reasonable terms. England would remain free, and keep the Empire, if it accepted German leadership on the continent. But Churchill decided to fight on.'

'He won.'

'You think so? Where is the Empire now? Where is Britain? We lost the leadership of the world. We let the Communists occupy half Europe. The Covenant was the work of brave men. They saw that Germany was our bulwark against Bolshevism. Fighting her was cutting our own throat. That is why they pledged that they supported the restoration of Edward VIII to the throne.'

'Is he the Duke of Westminster?'

'What? Of course not! The Duke of Windsor!'

Pryce-Jones had killed one of his own comrades barely an hour before, but her ignorance moved him more strongly.

'He abdicated in 1936. Manoeuvred out by Baldwin and the Jewish press. The Covenant was a loyal address to him to make himself ready to take up the throne again. It was intended to reassure the Germans that moves were underway to get rid of Churchill and bring peace.'

'And Hal's father was one of them.'

'He deceived me. I knew he was sympathetic to our cause. Many in the Secret Service are. They see the Soviets at work and don't have any illusions. But I had no idea he had a personal connection.'

'But why kill him? Why does that bloody thing matter so much?'

He picked up the Covenant.

'If I showed you these names, you would not believe the power they wield. Army officers. Judges. Politicians. Bankers. Industrialists. Household names, many of them. Of course, some have died or retired. But others are now more senior, more influential than ever. Even if only half of them join our cause, it will make all the difference.'

He was looking past her again, and now he throttled back on the engines. They drifted forward, slowing all the time. With a sick feeling, Clemency realised they had reached the far shore.

'You wait there, Miss White. You, come here.'

Shakily, Lucia rose to her feet.

'Take that rope and be ready to jump ashore. If you try anything, I will shoot. Do you understand?'

Lucia nodded, then walked to the front of the launch and picked up the mooring rope. She leapt onto a wooden jetty, much like the one they had left from, and wrapped the rope around a bollard. Part of Clemency wanted Lucia to run for it, but with Pryce-Jones standing ready only a few feet away, it was hopeless. She would be dead before she reached land.

'Now you.'

He waved Clemency onto the jetty to stand at Lucia's side. It wouldn't be here, she thought. But it wouldn't be long now.

'I want you to walk along the jetty and then turn left on the track. If one of you makes a run for it, the first shot will kill the other. You understand?'

They nodded, like errant schoolchildren in front of the headmaster. Then he waved them to turn and begin to walk. He followed a few steps behind. Out of reach.

There was enough light from the moon to pick out the path. There was a swathe of grass to their right, and then the forest began. But it would take them too long to make it. They would have to wait for a better chance.

But was there much longer?

Now Clemency could make out a wooden barn about fifty yards further on. Next to it was a long white vehicle. The ambulance that had brought them there.

'When we reach it,' she whispered to Lucia, 'he'll shoot us both.'

'Yes.'

In one word, Lucia said everything that Clemency was feeling. The anger and sadness, the fear and the frustration. The flicker of hope that, somehow, she might escape. The knowledge that there was a chance that one of them might survive, but not both.

This was what Pryce-Jones had planned. Shoot them here, then place them in the ambulance and drive them away to dispose of at his leisure. Their blood could be kicked into the dirt. Even if anyone heard the shots, then here, deep in the forest, they would assume it was a hunter.

She had to run for it. If she could lose herself in the shadows, there might be hope. Or maybe the unexpected. Make for the water, not the trees.

But for Lucia, dressed head to toe in white, there would be no hiding place. Clemency stopped.

'I'm so sorry. You were right. You should have run back at the chalet.'

Lucia stared at her, and then tears welled up in her eyes. Clemency's words had stripped away any illusions about their fate. She threw her arms around her and began to sob. Clemency held her, rubbing her back, saying soothing meaningless words, but her eyes were fixed on Pryce-Jones.

She licked her lips, trying to speak.

'Is this what you are fighting for? To shoot people in the back of the head? No trial? No justice?'

'It's war,' he replied, stiff with anger that he should be faced with this display of emotion.

'Who are your people? Are you Nazis?'

'Don't be absurd. We are patriots. Men who see the way the country's going. Who won't stand by and let the Communists take it over. Wilson's in their pay, you know. George Brown is being blackmailed by the KGB. The whole of Labour are compromised, and the Conservatives are not much better. That's why we have to be ready to fight back.'

'But you—'

'There's no time for this. And no point.' He checked the gun. 'Believe me, I am sorry. You're a plucky girl. Is there anything I can pass on to your people? I'll go to see them, of course, when I'm next in England. I'd like them to know you died a heroine. Maybe a medal would help. What do you think?'

At the thought of her home, she too began to cry.

'Anything? Well, don't worry. I'll think of something.'

'Drop the gun.'

Pryce-Jones froze.

'Put your hands up.'

A woman's voice, deep and commanding, coming from the trees.

'Cristina?'

Lucia had hardly spoken before Pryce-Jones had seized her and spun her round, so that she was between him and the woman emerging from the trees with a rifle at her hip.

'Don't come any closer.'

'If you hurt her, I will kill you.'

Instinctively, Clemency had backed away. Now it was too late to try and intervene, as Pryce-Jones's gun was jammed against the base of Lucia's skull. She thought of Hal, and bile rose in her throat.

'I'm sure we can resolve this,' Pryce-Jones called out, his voice as urbane as ever. 'I have something that appears to be of value to you. In return, you can let me be on my way.'

'Let her go. Then we talk.'

'My dear lady, I think we need to agree the rules first. You need to lay down your rifle, for one thing. I don't want you taking potshots at me as we drive off. Then I will walk to the ambulance with your, er, friend here. You will come along at a distance. Then I let her go. No doubt you will run back to the rifle, but by then I should be out of range. How does that sound?'

After a moment, Cristina crouched and laid down the rifle.

'Very good,' Pryce-Jones said. 'Now we can make some progress.'

He began to walk backwards, still using Lucia as protection. Cristina paced out a path in parallel but thirty feet from the track, moving further away from the rifle. Unsure what her role was, Clemency began to follow after them.

After they had covered fifty feet in this strange way, she began to believe they might survive. There was no way Pryce-Jones could kill all three of them without being killed himself. And none of them could do anything to him without losing at least one of their number.

If only they kept their heads, it was going to be all right. Pryce-Jones would have the Covenant, but that couldn't be helped. She would be happy to see a thousand Fascists recruited to his cause if it stopped him from killing Lucia.

They reached the ambulance. Hal produced the key and felt behind him until it was in the lock, his eyes on Cristina and Clemency.

He opened the door and eased himself back onto the seat, still holding Lucia. The Covenant went onto the passenger seat.

He turned to put the key in the ignition.

Clemency knew what Lucia was going to do, and shouted to her to stop. But as soon as the pistol moved from the back of her head, she twisted in his grip. Her hand flashed to her pocket and she had the blade in her hand and then slammed into his arm. He scrambled for the gun, but she had broken free and was running for her life.

He could have got out and shot her dead. But his mind, as always, was stronger than his emotion. She no longer mattered. Cristina was already running back for the rifle. So he slammed the door shut and started the car.

Then, with the sound of a gas fire being lit, but a hundred times louder, the car was filled with flames, incandescent, swirling and flickering. And in the midst of it, a black mannequin moving in jerks, trying to open the door.

Clemency ran forward. Then the heat hit her and she staggered, threw up her arm to shield her face. The windscreen blew out, showering the night with glittering fragments. Gouts of flame rose into the darkness and she thought of bonfire night and sparklers.

'The file!'

She heard Lucia's wail over the roar of the flames, but her eyes were still fixed on the blackened figure, not moving now, but one hand, one claw, still resting against the side window.

26

It was nearly dawn when they reached Bariloche, after taking a long route round to approach the town from the opposite direction to where the remains of the ambulance lay smouldering. They left the car that Cristina had hired outside the agency and walked to where a little crowd of passengers was waiting for the first bus to Puerto Montt, over the border into Chile. Clemency felt very conspicuous, very English, surrounded by the women in shawls and long wool skirts, the men in their shabby Sunday best suits, a few children who stared at her with solemn eyes.

The bus set off into the mountains, the old suspension jolting them so much that Clemency could not understand how the woman next to her managed to go off to sleep, her head on Clemency's shoulder, her mouth open, snoring gently. But then she woke with a start to find they were at the border.

After the hours crammed into the bus, it was a relief to step into the cold dry air and gaze out over the line of the Andes marching away north and south. The pale blue sky and the white of the mountain peaks was echoed in the flag of the Republic of Argentina snapping in the breeze. A hundred yards away was its counterpart: the red blue and white of the Republic of Chile.

Two uniformed men – perhaps police, or customs,

or border guards – were glancing through passports and poking at the mounds of luggage that the other travellers had clumped around their feet or which was still piled on the roof of the bus. Clemency was standing a little apart from them, because that's what an Englishwoman would do. After a while, they were waved back on to the bus. It ground forward along the road, across an invisible line, and the whole affair was repeated under the equally unresponsive gaze of the Chilean authorities.

Then the bus was on its way again. In the confusion, Clemency had found a seat opposite Cristina and Lucia. They had agreed to pretend they didn't know each other, but Clemency risked a stilted conversation in Spanish with Cristina about the times of trains to Santiago. But it wasn't the time or place to talk about what they had lived through and what would happen next. Soon Clemency was dozing again.

It was late in the afternoon when they reached Puerto Montt, a place of low wooden buildings with corrugated roofs at the end of a long inlet like a fjord, and Clemency had her first glimpse of the Pacific Ocean. The bus left them at the railway station and they booked two adjoining berths on the night train to the capital. The obliging conductor opened the connecting door, made up one of the beds for Lucia, who was coming down with a mild fever, and even produced a handful of aspirin. Soon Lucia was settled, looking a little better and managing a smile. That done, Cristina turned her gaze to Clemency, who realised with regret that explanations could no longer be put off. She wished she had asked the conductor for a drink. Instead, in a low voice she described as best she could the time from being drugged on the train. Lucia followed with detached interest, as if it were a bedtime story; but Cristina sat leaning forward eagerly, her eyes burning darkly.

'So there is nothing to link you or Lucia to the scene?'

'Nothing. But won't someone know that Lucia was involved? Or someone might recognise her from the train.'

'Perhaps. But she only met the man who first called himself Herr Schmidt, and then Dr Zoll. And he will say nothing.'

'When was this?'

'It began three months ago,' Cristina explained. 'Lucia was spending time with some of the Fascists, to see what she could learn.'

'These men assume we women are stupid and know nothing,' Lucia added. 'So, you sit and smile, and some flattery, and you learn.'

'I called her *la burra*. For her long ears.'

Cristina and Lucia exchanged a glance, and Clemency could not understand how she had ever missed the love that lay behind the affection and respect.

'The only difficulty was not to show what I felt inside,' Lucia went on. 'All my life, I have hated these people. My father and my mother, they came to Argentina because of the Fascists in my own country. They could not even work, for to be a teacher, you had to be a *Fasciti*.'

Even these few words tired Lucia and Cristina took up the story.

'One day a man came to the bar. He said his name was Schmidt and he wanted her help. A go-between. He had something of value to the British, and would she go to the Embassy to speak to them. For this, she would receive a part of the money. It was information on the British Fascists during the last war.

'To our surprise, Pryce-Jones said he wanted to gain the dossier very much. Lucia met him twice to talk about how much he would pay and how they would make the exchange. We believed he might wish to destroy the dossier, but if we could have time to copy it, this would not matter.'

'But he was tricking us...' Lucia added.

'To prove what he was selling was genuine, Schmidt gave Lucia a copy of one of the pages to show to Pryce-Jones. He also explained to her that the Covenant had been brought to Argentina by one of three men who had been part of the mission to meet the English Fascists in 1940. Their names were Werner, Ullmann and Zoll. But he brought Señor Linklater out from London to find the three men and take the dossier. At first, we thought it was to save the money. The British can be very mean. But now it is clear he wanted the dossier destroyed, and as the man who had it might have kept a copy, it was safer to kill him and burn all his papers.

'When you came, we wondered what was your role to be. That is why I asked you to meet Lucia. Then you went to Misiones and we heard rumours of a small war that Señor Linklater had begun.'

'But you knew it was Zoll all along?'

'No, not at all. You see, Zoll was already dead.'

'What?'

'He came to Argentina in 1947. But he was dead two years later. We were sure of that.'

'He died of radiation poisoning,' Lucia added. 'And cancers. He suffered very much.'

'The man who was Schmidt and then Zoll was in fact Neugarth. He was once a doctor, but he had to resign and became a criminal. Deceits and frauds, but always so convincing. Someone was using him as a front, just as he was using Lucia.'

'So…' Clemency tailed off. She'd known that everything Hal had told her on the train the Covenant had been a lie. But she hadn't realised that Zoll too was a fiction. And there were people behind Zoll – the ones who had traced her and Hal from Buenos Aires, provided the ambulance to meet the train, and planted the bomb that would have killed Zoll and Lucia as they left the chalet with the money, having killed Clemency and Hal.

'So now we know what happened,' Cristina said. 'But this is not what is most important. Did you read the Covenant?'

'Yes.'

'Can you remember any of the names? Any proofs?'

'It wouldn't matter if I did or not. The whole thing was a fake.'

'What do you mean?'

Now that she had finally voiced her suspicions, Clemency became more confident.

'The Covenant was a forgery. The whole thing was made up.'

'You're lying!' Cristina sprang to her feet, seeming to fill the cabin. 'It cannot be. You are trying to protect your people.'

Clemency said nothing, and Cristina's accusing words faded away.

'I am sorry,' she said in a while. 'But are you sure? A fake?'

'We were fooled. All of us. Me, Hal, Pryce-Jones.

You, Lucia. We all wanted to believe it. But it was a trap, and we all stepped into it.'

'Do you know who set this trap?'

'Oh, yes. I know who. And why.'

They fell silent. From outside came the voice of the conductor, then a long and stylish whistle, and the train began to move.

27

However many times Jeremy Parsons totalled them up, the numbers didn't agree. A difference of 32 pesos. A stupid amount. He could put his hand in his pocket and make up the difference. But these were the monthly accounts for the Embassy, and they had to match. To the auditors, putting in his own money in would be as bad as stealing. And now here was Stephens to bother him, though he'd said he mustn't be disturbed.

'What young lady?' he snapped. 'Tell her she needs the consulate.'

'She asked for the Head of Chancellery.'

'Really?' Odd she'd know the technical term for the political side of the Embassy. And Stephens was going to stand there all day until he took over this problem. That was the problem with ex-NCOs. Once they decided something was a matter for an officer, they wouldn't shift. More bloody-minded than any union shop steward.

'Very well. Show her in.'

There were only three diplomats at the British Embassy in Santiago, and with the Ambassador home on leave and Colonel Collins far to the south, reviewing the security arrangements at the consulate in Valparaiso, Parsons was feeling overworked and underappreciated.

'Miss White? How can I help?'

She sat down, quite young, very reserved, decent clothes if a little travel-worn, and black smudges beneath her eyes.

'Could you send a telegram for me? To ACTOR.'

As he said later to Colonel Collins, if she'd asked him to sell her an elephant, he couldn't have been any more surprised.

'To ACTOR?' he repeated. How on earth could she know the code for SIS? 'Er... could I see this telegram?'

'I haven't written it yet. I thought there was a chance I might be picked up by the Chileans.'

'Yes. Quite. Very sensible, I'm sure. Could I ask if you have some form of identification? We're being particularly cautious at the moment,' he added, almost apologetically. 'After the incident in Argentina.'

'What incident was that?' There was a new tension in her voice.

'One of our diplomats was killed in a car bomb. Marxist terrorists, they say.'

'I haven't seen the papers. Was it Jacob Pryce-Jones?'

'Yes. Did you know him?'

'I saw it happen.'

◊

They had parted at the Alameda station, the grey half-light matching their mood. Clemency had wanted them to stay in Chile, but Cristina was sure that she and Lucia would not be on any watch list and could risk a flight to Montevideo and then the ferry to Buenos Aires.

'The sooner we are home, the better,' she had said in her usual, decisive way. 'I do not think the S.I.D.E. will want to look too closely into this.'

But that was not Clemency's fear. They would not be arrested this week or this month, but they were returning to a country where the tide of Fascism was rising. They would be involved in resisting, and with their courage and commitment, they would never be safe. One day there would be a knock on the door in the early hours and they would vanish into a detention centre. Or another car bomb, leaving them like the horror she had seen on the shores of the lake.

The only thing she was sure of was that she would never see them again.

They held her tight in turn, so that Clemency's English reserve gave way to Latin tears.

'What do you plan to do to him?' Cristina asked.

'Make sure it never happens again.'

For all her concern for Clemency, Cristina still nodded approvingly. If the man had been standing there with them, and Cristina had a knife in her hand, she would have killed him without compunction. Clemency, though, was thinking of a different way.

She had seen them onto a bus to the airport, and then turned to find a taxi to the Embassy. Settling back in the seat, watching the unfamiliar city pass by, exhaustion had overwhelmed her. She had begun to compose the telegram in her mind, but it was hard to concentrate.

Now, with the wheels in motion – so slow, but picking up speed with every hour – she was forcing herself to concentrate. There were cables from Buenos Aires, demanding more details, more explanation. There were telegrams marked FLASH and EYES ONLY from Swan in London, even more unwelcome as she had to decode them herself, and the groups of letters kept dancing before her eyes, so she made mistakes and came up with meaningless jumbles.

Parsons was looking almost sorry for her as he brought in another request from BA.

'Couldn't I just call them?' she asked, eyeing the phone on the desk.

'Oh no,' he replied. 'Apparently the Soviets have a tap on the phone lines here. I don't know how we found out, but it means we can't use it for anything sensitive.'

'Really?' Clemency said, her tiredness slipping away. 'How inconvenient.'

Parsons glanced at his watch.

'Look, I have to go off for a couple of hours. Will you be all right here? Stephens can get you anything you need. Tea and so on. Or a bite to eat.'

She assured him she would be fine, and stood at the window, watching until he had hurried down the stairs and into his car, standing protected behind the high gates of the Embassy compound. Then she picked up the phone.

'Could you get me the British Embassy in Buenos Aires? It's rather urgent.'

◊

There was a secure line to the consulate in Valparaiso, and so Parsons could report the day's events, and ventilate some of his feelings, to Colonel Collins.

'I got Stephens to drive her out to the airport,' he said. 'First thing she does is pick up her London ticket from the BOAC desk, and then exchange it for one with LAN Chile to Quito.'

'Really?' Collins seemed to think it amusing. 'These people are extraordinary, aren't they? Not that it's our problem if she's fiddling her expenses.'

'And on the way, she stopped at the Bank of London and South America. I know the manager there socially. He tells me she cashed in some traveller's cheques and then had the lot wired to a hotel in Cuba. $5,000.'

'Just be grateful she's off your hands,' Collins replied soothingly. 'The last thing you want is to have anything to do with these cloak and dagger types.'

'Oh, quite. I have my suspicions that she dragged poor Pryce-Jones into one of their little capers. Look what happened to him.'

28

Clemency woke to find it was night and they were touching down in Ecuador. She had four hours in the airport lounge, where she drank coffee but couldn't eat anything. She chatted up the Iberia booking clerk until he bought her story, and then she was on the move again.

Dawn came over the forests of Costa Rica. At San José, the plane picked up a handful of passengers, walking across the tarmac in the early light. And there he was, incongruous in his roll-neck sweater, coat over one arm and briefcase in the other, the very picture of an internationally renowned author.

The stewardess led Sorokin to his seat, and when he saw who he was next to, he froze. Did he think that maybe this was a trap? That she might draw out a gun and try to kill him in revenge for Hal's death? She stood, so he could see there was no weapon beneath her slim sheath dress. He managed to drag a smile onto his face and came up to her, kissing her on both cheeks in the Russian manner.

'This is a delight,' he said. 'Somehow I knew we would meet again.'

'So did I,' she said sweetly. 'Are you going all the way to Madrid?'

'Just to Havana,' he replied, looking around furtively to see if there were any other source of danger. She almost felt sorry for him. He would never make a secret agent, however much he might try.

'I would say that it's a small world, but to a writer of your eminence, clichés must be painful.'

'They can be useful,' he said abstractedly, deciding that taking his seat would be less trouble than protesting that he had to be moved.

'How was San José?'

'What? Oh, delightful. A very cultured country. My thoughts on the role of the artist in today's troubled world situation were particularly well-received.'

'I'm glad.'

'And you? How is…?'

He fell sympathetically silent.

'As you can see, I'm on my own,' she said. 'I'm sorry to say I've been jilted, if you know the word. My so-called fiancé disappeared, leaving me in the lurch. So I'm going home. Sadder and wiser.'

'I am most sorry to hear that,' Sorokin said formally.

The stewardess came round with a tray of champagne. Sorokin reached for his glass eagerly. Clemency took one, but then offered it to him untouched once his was drained.

'You are most kind,' he said. 'Flying does not agree with me.'

'We'll be fine,' she said soothingly.

'I will believe you once we are back on the ground.'

Sorokin took out his cigarette case and offered her one. She pointed to the no smoking sign lit up above their heads. He sighed and put the case away.

'Do you remember,' she began, 'at that dinner party, saying you sometimes wondered what it would be like if one of your characters came to life and met you in person?'

'I do. You replied that it would be every bit as fascinating if you were to meet whoever had written your life story.'

'That's why I'm here. Because for those weeks I was in Argentina, you wrote the story, didn't you? Right from the start.'

Perhaps the drink was doing him some good. He leaned closer and spoke in a low voice, drowned to those around by the sound of the engines.

'This is so odd,' he said thoughtfully. 'So many times I have written the scene in which the hero reveals the method by which the villains are defeated. Always I have thought to myself, why would he do this? What is to be gained? In real life, this is not how it is. Yet I find I wish to tell you everything. So, I am at your disposal. Ask me, and I will answer.'

Clemency swallowed, a little sickened. To him, it was still a game, a puzzle. Then again, he hadn't seen Hal's brains blown out, or Pryce-Jones incinerated.

'I don't have any questions,' she replied, trying to keep her voice steady. 'I know everything. You had contacts in the KGB. They'd helped you with the background for your stories. Then they thought – or maybe you suggested it – you could use your creative skills to do a little more for Mother Russia. You could help them design a whole operation. You'd write the script, and it would be acted out in real life. There never was a Covenant. It's all propaganda. You invented it to discredit the British establishment.'

Sorokin made a show of finding the idea amusing.

'Go on.'

'You were clever enough to use the truth wherever you could. To make it plausible. Unfortunately, the British thought that a conspiracy to bring back

Edward VIII was all too believable.'

'You are guessing. But your guess happens to be correct,' he added graciously. 'It began in a discussion over lunch in the canteen in Dzinski Street. I was there to see for myself the place and discuss some of the work for a book, but we came to talking about whether the artist could use their insight to understand better their opponents in the Western intelligence services.

'I was bold – perhaps it was the vodka – and claimed that I could develop an operation that would employ the psychology of the West and win a victory for Russia. Then, my idle boast became an operational directive. And here we are.'

She nodded, as if admiring anything done well.

'The Covenant was one of my finest works,' he went on. 'The task was not easy, you understand. It had to tell of things that the British believed to be true, or close enough to the truth that they could not dismiss it. That way, they would have to gain it and destroy it. And the Fascist leanings of your Royal Family was a perfect seed for the story.'

'The names were convincing,' she said. 'Pryce-Jones must have known a number of them and could imagine them doing exactly that.'

'This is true. We looked through our files of the English proto-fascists going back to the War and before. We could have had more than fifty names on the list, believe me,' he added with a chuckle.

'Why Argentina?'

'The important element was that the Covenant had to have the right provenance. You know the meaning? As for a work of art? The value is that you know where it has been, so that you know it is not a fake. In this case, Argentina was ideal. Where was more likely than for such a document to emerge there?

'The plotting had to be simple. We do not have elaborate resources in South America, and to bring in agents would be to invite the interest of the Argentinian intelligence service, who can be very thorough. Therefore, I created the character of the Nazi criminal who had run out of the money they had brought with them from Germany and wished to sell the dossier to the British. Maliakov recruited a doctor called Neugarth to play this part, and he in turn approached Lucia Sabatini because it was known that she had contacts amongst the German exiles. She was therefore an ideal go-between. She was completely taken in by Neugarth and because she stood to make a large amount of money herself, she was very persuasive. Neugarth fed to the British, through her, enough to make them hungry for more.'

'But you couldn't have known that she even existed.'

'I conceived the idea of her,' Semenov replied. 'The girl Sabatini was no more than an actress cast into a part that I had written. You see, the man to approach at the Embassy was Pryce-Jones. So English, so proper. So repressed. I imagined the contrast with this flashing-eyed beauty, with her sleek black hair and her long legs. He would hate her, yet be drawn to her, and so my plot would unfold.'

'But you didn't want her to just sell him the Covenant.'

'Ah! Very good! You are ahead of me, I see. Yes, for if the Covenant on which we had lavished so much care – the documents so carefully forged, cross-checked against facts that could be proved, and then aged with the best skills of the laboratories of the GRU – if we sold it to Pryce-Jones, it would never reach the outside world. It would sow suspicion, and perhaps wreck a few careers, but it would not have the world-wide attention which we wanted. You see, you British will always cover up a scandal. At this, you are the best in the world.'

'Is that why you sent us after the false leads – Ullmann and Werner?'

'In part. The more time and effort to find the Covenant, the more it must be worth. But it was also so that there would be a trail of destruction in your wake. And in that, we were well-served by the man Linklater. So very... *vigorous*. Gun battles. Arson. Burglary. Though I believe that you were involved as well.'

'Why did you want all this destruction?'

'So that the finale should not come out of the blue. Already there has been one gun battle. Another will be no surprise. The police come. What do they find? A Nazi and his beautiful but deadly assistant dead in a burned-out car. An agent of the famous British Secret Service and his may I say equally beautiful but deadly assistant, murdered in a lakeside chalet.'

'And they would find the Covenant.'

'Exactly. Then there will be a tip-off to one of America's most respected journalists, who happens to be in the country. He will find it easy to bribe a policeman to obtain the Covenant. It will cost him a lot, but he will be repaid many times over by the story that he will write. A story that will go around the world.'

Sorokin was leaning forward, eager, insistent that she should admire his work.

'As I say, the scene will tell the story. It has everything that the modern decadent Western mind wants. Crime, betrayal, sex and death. And then, when the excitement might be about to fade, comes the secret that they died fighting over – the man who was once the King of England making a pact with Adolf Hitler to attack the Soviet Union.'

He drained his glass of champagne and looked hopefully down the aisle, but the stewardesses were gossiping and he could not catch their eye. His pleasure in retelling the story quickly evaporated.

'Tell me,' he said abruptly. 'What happened in the chalet?'

'You don't know?'

'I know what happened, but not why. The girl Sabatini – did she change sides? Was it for money? And you? Why are you here? For knowledge? I think you are one of those who must know the answer, whatever the danger.'

'Perhaps. But aren't you the one who's in danger? You will have a lot to explain away on your return. I don't imagine the KGB look kindly on failure.'

'Failure? You think so? One of your best agents is dead. A valuable piece taken from the board. Add in Pryce-Jones and the harm to your relations with the Argentinians, and I think we would call it a victory. And what move is now open to you? Tell the Argentines the truth? That you were operating on their territory, hunting Nazis, just like the Israelis? That was part of my thinking. A safety device, if you like. Once you were committed, you were in the wrong with your hosts and could not cry foul.'

'I see that now,' Clemency said, a little crestfallen.

'This is a game for men,' he said, placing his hand on her knee. 'I hope you will not involve yourself again. I would hate for you to be one of the pieces sacrificed, the next time I play.'

Having relieved himself of this sentiment, he rose and went to the toilet. She stood and reached for her overnight bag, sliding his coat out of the way as she did so. By the time he returned, she was unfolding a week-old copy of the *New York Times*.

Now the spell was broken. Sorokin sat in silence, perhaps regretting his openness. Or maybe it was the effects of the champagne wearing off, or the sound of the flaps going down as they approached the airport at Havana.

But once they were down and the plane was sitting on the apron outside the terminal building, the door open and the tropical air taking the edge off the air-conditioned chill of the cabin, he could not resist a last exchange.

'Tell your Mr Swan from me, I much enjoyed our game.'

'I'll do that,' she said meekly. 'And good luck with your talk tonight.'

She could have bitten off her tongue. Now he would ask himself how she knew what his plans were, and then it would be clear this was no accidental meeting, and he would become suspicious.

But he only smiled.

'It will be the highlight of my trip. You would be surprised how many copies I sell here. Also, Cuba is as true to the principles of Marxism-Leninism as Moscow – but with better weather!'

She guessed this was a line he planned to use that night. But she was still nervous as he kissed her hand, collected his belongings and made his way to the exit. A man in a badly-cut suit, with the blank eyes of the professional watcher, fell into step behind him.

She rubbed her eyes. It had been so hard not to tell

him the truth. She had wanted so much to see his face
fall when she explained the trap she had sprung. The
telephone call to the Embassy in BA, confirming that
she would next make contact with Sorokin on his
flight to Havana, to the considerable confusion of
the unknown official at the other end, but hopefully
making sense to the Soviet eavesdroppers. The list of
areas of interest that SIS wanted Sorokin to go after
once he was back in Moscow, that she had typed up in
the Embassy in Santiago and which was now nestling
in his coat pocket. The $5,000 waiting at his hotel.

Now he was walking from the steps of the plane
towards the terminal. Jaunty. She half-expected him to
turn and wave to her. But there were two men in white
shirts and dark glasses walking to meet him, showing
him their identification, and pointing to a black saloon
car pulling up close to them on the tarmac. Perhaps they
would pretend to be a welcoming committee from the
Ministry of Culture. Or perhaps they wouldn't bother.

Sorokin was protesting, waving his arms, pointing
back towards the plane.

She'd known the risk. They could hold the plane,
take her off for questioning, and her ruse would soon
be exposed. She had gambled that they would not
want to drag a British citizen off a Spanish plane. And
there would be no need. They had all the evidence
they needed to put Sorokin in front of a firing squad,
without drawing her into it.

Sorokin tried to break free. In a moment, a single jab
to the ribs, and he was bent over and being half-helped,
half-pushed into the car. One of them produced a black
hood and slipped it over his head. The men climbed in
and at once it drove off and out of sight.

She lay back in the seat.

'Señorita?'

She opened her eyes. The stewardess wanted her to do up her seat belt. The plane was already moving towards the runway, ready to leave. Then she handed Clemency the menu.

'We have everything except the fish.'

'I won't want to eat, thank you,' Clemency replied, handing it back. 'Just to rest.'

'Of course. I will make sure you are not disturbed.'

A few moments later she returned with a blanket and a pillow. But the English girl in Seat 7A was already asleep.

THE END

Clemency White will return in
COME SPY WITH ME